The Jumping Frog And 18 Other Stories

By

MARK TWAIN

Published 2000
The Book Tree
Escondido, CA

Printed on Acid-Free Paper

The Jumping Frog and 18 Other Stories
ISBN 1-58509-200-2

Published by
The Book Tree
Post Office Box 724
Escondido, CA 92033

CONTENTS

INTRODUCTION

This collection of Mark Twain stories has not been in print for many years and in this regard seems to be a new and rare collection. For example, out of the nineteen short stories contained here we found only two (*The Jumping Frog* and *Corn-Pone Opinions*) that were included in a larger collection commonly available called *Great Short Works of Mark Twain.*

The Jumping Frog was the story that launched Mark Twain's career. He was loitering around the Angel's Camp mining town in California and was told the story in a worn out saloon by a bald-headed local who relayed the story to him in a deadpan tone of voice, with no hint of excitement or humor. Twain wrote out the story and sent it to a humorist friend in New York, and it wound up being published in the prestigious *Saturday Press.* The story was copied and reprinted by newspapers throughout Europe and America, and Twain was on his way.

These are great representative stories of Twain. They should make a good addition for collectors, libraries, or to classroom programs wishing to study the art of short story writing. More importantly, this rare volume should serve as a colorful and exciting addition to those who appreciate Twain's wit and wisdom.

Paul Tice

THE JUMPING FROG

In English. Then in French. Then clawed back into a civilized language once more by patient, unremunerated toil.

Even a criminal is entitled to fair play; and certainly when a man who has done no harm has been unjustly treated, he is privileged to do his best to right himself. My attention has just been called to an article some three years old in a French Magazine entitled, *Revue des Duex Mondes* (Review of Some Two Worlds), wherein the writer treats of "Les Humoristes Americaines" (These Humorists Americans). I am one of these humorists Americans dissected by him, and hence the complaint I am making.

This gentleman's article is an able one (as articles go in the French, where they always tangle up everything to that degree that when you start into a sentence you never know whether you are going to come out alive or not). It is a very good article, and the writer says all manner of kind and complimentary things about me—for which I am sure I thank him with all my heart; but then why should he go and spoil all his praise by one unlucky experiment? What I refer to is this: he says my Jumping Frog is a funny story, but still he can't see why it should ever really convulse any one with laughter—and straightway proceeds to translate it into French in order to prove to his nation that there is nothing so very extravagantly funny about it. Just there is where my complaint originates. He has not translated it at all; he has simply mixed it all up; it is no more like the Jumping Frog when he gets through with it than I am like a meridian of longitude. But my mere assertion is not proof; wherefore I print the French version, that all may see that I do not speak falsely; furthermore, in order that even the unlettered may know my injury and give me their compassion, I have been at infinite pains and trouble to retranslate this French version back into English; and to tell the truth, I have well-nigh worn myself out at it, having scarcely rested from my work during five days and nights. I cannot speak the French language, but I can translate very well, though not fast, I being self-educated. I ask the reader to run his eye over the original English version of the

Jumping Frog, and then read the French or my retranslation, and kindly take notice how the Frechman has riddled the grammar. I think it is the worst I ever saw; and yet the French are called a polished nation. If I had a boy that put sentences together as they do, I would polish him to some purpose. Without further introduction, the Jumping Frog, as I originally wrote it, was as follows [after it will be found the French version, and after the latter my retranslation from the French]:

THE NOTORIOUS JUMPING FROG OF CALAVERAS[1] COUNTY

In compliance with the request of a friend of mine, who wrote me from the East, I called on good-natured, garrulous old Simon Wheeler, and inquired after my friend's friend, Leonidas W. Smiley, as requested to do, and I hereunto append the result. I have a lurking suspicion that *Leonidas W.* Smiley is a myth; that my friend never knew such a personage; and that he only conjectured that if I asked old Wheeler about him, it would remind him of his infamous *Jim* Smiley, and he would go to work and bore me to death with some exasperating reminiscence of him as long and as tedious as it should be useless to me. If that was the design, it succeeded.

I found Simon Wheeler dozing comfortably by the barroom stove of the dilapidated tavern in the decayed mining camp of Angel's, and I noticed that he was fat and baldheaded, and had an expression of winning gentleness and simplicity upon his tranquil countenance. He roused up, and gave me good day. I told him that a friend of mine had commissioned me to make some inquires about a cherished companion of his boyhood named *Leonidas W.* Smiley—*Rev. Leonidas W.* Smiley, a young minister of the Gospel, whom he had heard was at one time a resident of Angel's Camp. I added that if Mr. Wheeler could tell me anything about this Rev. Leonidas W. Smiley, I would feel under many obligations to him.

Simon Wheeler backed me into a corner and blockaded me there with his chair, and then sat down and reeled off the monotonous narrative which follows this paragraph. He never smiled, he never frowned, he never changed his voice from the gentle-flowing key to which he tuned his initial sentence, he never betrayed the slightest suspicion of enthusiasm; but all through the interminable narrative there ran a vein of impressive earnestness and sincerity, which showed me plainly that, so far

[1] Pronounced Cal-e-*va*-ras.

from his imagining that there was anything ridiculous or funny about his story, he regarded it as a really important matter, and admired its two heroes as men of transcendent genius in *finesse.* I let him go on in his own way, and never interrupted him once.

"Rev. Leonidas W. H'm, Reverend Le—well, there was a feller here once by the name of *Jim* Smiley, in the winter of '49—or maybe it was the spring of '50—I don't recollect exactly, somehow, though what makes me think it was one or the other is because I remember the big flame warn't finished when he first come to the camp; but anyway, he was the curiousest man about always betting on anything that turned up you ever see, if he could get anybody to bet on the other side; and if he couldn't he'd change sides. Any way that suited the other man would suit *him*—any way just so's he got a bet, *he* was satisfied. But still he was lucky, uncommon lucky; he most always come out winner. He was always ready and laying for a chance; there couldn't be no solit'ry thing mentioned but that feller'd offer to bet on it, and take ary side you please, as I was just telling you. If there was a horse-race, you'd find him flush or you'd find him busted at the end of it; if there was a dog-fight, he'd bet on it; if there was a cat-fight, he'd bet on it; if there was a chicken-fight, he'd bet on it; why, if there was two birds setting on a fence, he would bet you which one would fly first; or if there was a camp-meeting, he would be there reg'lar to bet on Parson Walker, which he judged to be the best exhorter about here, and so he was too, and a good man. If he even see a straddle-bug start to go anywheres, he would bet you how long it would take him to get to—to wherever he was going to, and if you took him up, he would foller that straddle-bug to Mexico but what he would find out where he was bound for and how long he was on the road. Lots of boys here has seen that Smiley, and can tell you about him. Why, it never made no difference to *him*—he'd bet on *any* thing—the dangdest feller. Parson Walker's wife laid very sick once, for a good while, and it seemed as if they warn't going to save her; but one morning he come in, and Smiley up and asked him how she was, and he said she was considerable better—thank the Lord for his inf'nite mercy—and coming on so smart that with the blessing of Prov'dence she'd get well yet; and Smiley, before he thought, says, 'Well, I'll resk two-and-a-halt she don't anyway.'

"Thish-yer Smiley had a mare—the boys called her the fifteen-minute nag, but that was only in fun, you know, because of course she was faster than that—and he used to win money on that horse, for all she was so slow and always had the asthma, or the distemper, or the consumption, or something of that kind. They used to give her two or three hundred yards' start, and then pass her under way; but always at the fag end of the race she'd get excited and desperate like, and come cavorting and straddling up, and scattering her legs around limber, sometimes in the air, and sometimes out to one side among the fences, and kicking up m-o-r-e dust and raising m-o-r-e racket with her coughing and sneezing and blowing her nose—and *always* fetch up at the stand just about a neck ahead, as near as you could cipher it down.

"And he had a little small bull-pup, that to look at him you'd think he warn't worth a cent but to set around and look ornery and lay for a chance to steal something. But as soon as money was up on him he was a different dog; his under-jaw'd begin to stick out like the fo'castle of a steamboat, and his teeth would uncover and shine like the furnaces. And a dog might tackle him and bully-rag him, and bite him, and throw him over his shoulder two or three times, and Andrew Jackson—which was the name of the pup—Andrew Jackson would never let on but what *he* was satisfied, and hadn't expected nothing else—and the bets being doubled and doubled on the other side all the time, till the money was all up; and then all of a sudden he would grab that other dog jest by the j'int of his hind leg and freeze to it—not chaw, you understand, but only just grip and hang on till they throwed up the sponge, if it was a year. Smiley always come out winner on that pup, till he harnessed a dog once that didn't have no hind legs, because they'd been sawed off in a circular saw, and when the thing had gone along far enough, and the money was all up, and he come to make a snatch for his pet holt, he see in a minute how he'd been imposed on, and how the other dog had him in the door, so to speak, and he 'peared surprised, and then he looked sorter discouraged-like, and didn't try no more to win the fight, and so he got shucked out bad. He give Smiley a look as much as to say his heart was broke, and it was *his* fault, for putting up a dog that hadn't no hind legs for him to take holt of, which was his main dependence in a fight, and then he limped off a piece and laid down and died. It was a good pup, was that Andrew Jackson, and would have made a name for hisself if he'd lived, for the stuff was in him and he had genius—I know, because he hadn't no opportunities to speak of, and it don't stand to reason that a dog could make such a fight as he could under them circumstances if he hadn't no talent. It always makes me feel sorry when I think of that last fight of his'n, and the way it turned out.

"Well, thish-yer Smiley had rat-tarriers, and chicken cocks, and tomcats and all them kind of things, till you couldn't rest, and you couldn't fetch nothing for him to bet on but he'd match you. He ketched a frog one day, and took him home, and said he cal'lated to educate him; and so he never done nothing for three months but set in his back yard and learn that frog to jump. And you bet you he *did* learn him, too. He'd give him a little punch behind, and the next minute you'd see that frog whirling in the air like a doughnut — see him turn one summerset, or maybe a couple, if he got a good start, and come down flat-footed and all right, like a cat. He got him up so in the matter of ketching flies, and kep' him in practice so constant, that he'd nail a fly every time as fur as he could see him. Smiley said all a frog wanted was education, and he could do 'most anything—and I believe him. Why, I've seen him set Dan'l Webster down here on this floor—Dan'l Webster was the name of the frog—and sing out, 'Flies, Dan'l, flies!' and quicker'n you could wink he'd spring straight up and snake a fly off'n the counter there, and hop down on the floor ag'in as solid as a gob of mud, and fall to scratching the side of his head with his hind foot as indifferent as if he hadn't no idea he'd been doin' any more'n any frog might do. You never see a frog so modest and straightfor'ard as he was, for all he was so gifted. And when it come to fair and square jumping on a dead level, he could get over more ground at one straddle than any animal of his breed you ever see. Jumping on a dead level was his strong suit, you understand; and when it come to that, Smiley would ante up money on him as long as he had a red. Smiley was monstrous proud of his frog, and well he might be, for fellers that had traveled and been everywheres all said he laid over any frog that ever *they* see.

"Well, Smiley kep' the beast in a little lattice box, and he used to fetch him down-town sometimes and lay for a bet. One day a feller—a stranger in the camp, he was—come acrost him with his box, and says:

" 'What might it be that you've got in the box?'

"And Smiley says, sorter indifferent-like, 'It might be a parrot or it might be a canary, maybe, but it ain't—it's only just a frog.'

"And the feller took it, and looked at it careful, and turned it round this way and that, and says, 'H'm—so 'tis. Well, what's *he* good for?'

" 'Well,' Smiley says, easy and careless, 'he's good enough for *one* thing, I should judge—he can outjump any frog in Calaveras County.'

"The feller took the box again, and took another long, particular look, and give it back to Smiley, and says, very deliberate, 'Well,' he says, 'I don't see no p'ints about that frog that's any better'n any other frog.'

" 'Maybe you don't,' Smiley says. 'Maybe you understand frogs and maybe you don't understand 'em; maybe you've had experience and maybe you ain't only a amature, as it were. Anyways, I've got *my* opinion, and I'll resk forty dollars that he can outjump any frog in Calaveras County.'

"And the feller studied a minute, and then says, kinder sadlike, 'Well, I'm only a stranger here, and I ain't got no frog; but if I had a frog, I'd bet you.'

"And then Smiley says, 'That's all right—that's all right—if you'll hold my box a minute, I'll go and get you a frog.' And so the feller took the box and put up his forty dollars along with Smiley's, and set down to wait.

"So he set there a good while thinking and thinking to himself, and then he got the frog out and pried his mouth open and took a teaspoon and filled him full of quail-shot—filled him pretty near up to his chin—and set him on the floor. Smiley he went to the swamp and slopped around in the mud for a long time, and finally he ketched a frog, and fetched him in, and give him to this feller, and says:

" 'Now, if you're ready, set him alongside of Dan'l, with his fore paws just even with Dan'l's, and I'll give the word.' Then he says, 'One—two—three—*git!*' and him and the feller touched up the frogs from behind, and the new frog hopped off lively, but Dan'l give a heave, and hysted up his shoulders—so—like a Frenchman, but it warn't no use—he couldn't budge; he was planted as solid as a church, and he couldn't no more stir than if he was anchored out. Smiley was a good deal surprised, and he was disgusted too, but he didn't have no idea what the matter was, of course.

"The feller took the money and started away; and when he was going out at the door, he sorter jerked his thumb over his shoulder—so—at Dan'l, and says again, very deliberate, 'Well,' he says, '*I* don't see no p'ints about that frog that's any better'n any other frog.'

"Smiley he stood scratching his head and looking down at Dan'l a long time, and at last he says, 'I do wonder what in the nation that frog throw'd off for—I wonder if there ain't something the matter with him—he 'pears to look mighty baggy, somehow.' And he katched Dan'l by the nap of the neck, and hefted him, and says, 'Why blame my cats if he don't weigh five pound!' and turned him upside down and he belched out a double handful of shot. And then he see how it was, and he was the maddest man—he set the frog down and took out after that feller, but he never ketched him. And——"

[Here Simon Wheeler heard his name called from the front yard, and got up to see what was wanted.] And turning to me as he moved away, he said: "Just set where you are, stranger, and rest easy—I ain't going to be gone a second."

But, by your leave, I did not think that a continuation of the history of the enterprising vagabond *Jim* Smiley would be likely to afford me much information concerning the Rev. *Leonidas W*. Smiley, and so I started away.

At the door I met the sociable Wheeler returning, and he buttonholed me and recommenced:

"Well, thish-yer Smiley had a yaller one-eyed cow that didn't have no tail, only just a short stump like a bannanner, and——"

However, lacking both time and inclination, I did not wait to hear about the afflicted cow, but took my leave.

Now let the learned look upon this picture and say if iconoclasm[1] can further go:

LA GRENOUILLE SAUTEUSE DU COMTÉ DE CALAVERAS
From the *Revue des Deux Mondes,* of July 15th, 1872.

"—Il y avait une fois ici un individu connu sous le nom de Jim Smiley: c'était dans l'hiver de 49, peut-être bien au printemps de 50, je ne me rappelle pas exactement. Ce qui me fait croire que c'était l'un ou l'autre, c'est que je me souviens que le grand bief n'était pas achevé lorsqu'il arriva au camp pour la premiére fois, mais de toutes façons il était l'homme de plus friand de paris qui se pût voir, pariant sur tout ce qui se présentait, quand il pouvait trouver un adversaire, et, quand il n'en trouvait pas, il passait du côté opposé. Tout ce qui convenait à l'autre lui convenait; pourvu qu'il eût un pari, Smiley était satisfait. Et il avait une chance! une chance inouïe: presque toujours il gagnait. Il faut dire qu'il était toujours prêt à s'exposer qu'on ne pouvait mentionner la moindre chose sans que ce gaillard offrît de parier là-dessus n'importe quoi et de

[1] The shattering of idols, or of cherished beliefs.

prendre le côté que l'on voudrait, comme je vous le disais tout à l'heure. S'il y avait des courses, vous le trouviez riche ou ruiné à la fin; s'il y avait un combat de chiens, il apportait son enjeu; il l'apportait pour un combat de chats, pour un combat de coqs;—parbleu! si vous aviez vu deux oiseaux sur une haie, il vous aurait offert de parier lequel s'envolerait le premier, et, s'il y avait *meeting* au camp, il venait parier régulièrement pour le curé Walker, qu'il jugeait être le meilleur prédicateur des environs, et qui l'était en effet, et un brave homme. Il aurait rencontré une punaise de bois en chemin, qu'il aurait parié sur le temps qu'il lui faudrait pour aller où elle voudrait aller, et si vous l'aviez pris au mot, il aurait suivi la punaise jusqu'au Mexique, sans se soucier d'aller si loin, ni du temps qu'il y perdrait. Une fois la femme du curé Walker fut très malade pendant longtemps, il semblait qu'on ne la sauverait pas; mais un matin le curé arrive, et Smiley lui demande comment ella va, et il dit qu'elle est bien mieux, grâce à l'infinie miséricorde, tellement mieux qu'avec la bénédiction de la Providence elle s'en tirerait, et voilá que, sans y penser, Smiley répond:—Eh bien! je gage deux et demi qu'elle mourra tout de même.

"Ce Smiley avait une jument que les gars appelaient le bidet du quart d'heure, mais seulement pour plaisanter, vous comprenez, parce que, bien entendu, elle était plus *vite* que ça! Et il avait coutume de gagner de l'argent avec cette bête, quoiqu'elle fût poussive, cornarde, toujours prise d'asthme, de coliques ou de consomption, ou de quelque chose d'approchant. On lui donnait 2 ou 300 *yards* au départ, puis on la dépassait sans peine; mais jamais à la fin elle ne manquait de s'échauffer, de s'exaspérer, et elle arrivait, s'écartant, se défendant, ses jambes grêles en l'air devant les obstacles, quelquefois les évitant et faisant avec cela plus de poussière qu'aucun cheval, plus de bruit surtout avec ses éternumens et reniflemens—crac! elle arrivait donc toujours première d'une tête, aussi juste qu'on peut le mesurer. Et il avait un petit bouledogue qui, à le voir, ne valait pas un sou; on aurait cru que parier contre lui c'était voler, tant il était ordinaire; mais aussitôt les enjeux faits, il devenait un autre chien. Sa mâchoire inférieure commençait à ressortir comme un gaillard d'avant, ses dents se découvraient brillantes commes des fournaises, et un chien pouvait le taquiner, l'exciter le mordre, le jeter deux ou trois fois par-dessus son épaule, André Jackson, c'était le nom du chien, André Jackson prenait cela tranquillement, comme s'il ne se fût jamais attendu à autre chose, et quand les paris étaient doublés et redoublés contre lui, il vous saisissait l'autre chien juste à l'articulation de la jambe de derrière, et il ne la lâchait plus, non pas qu'il la mâchât, vous concevez, mais il s'y serait tenu pendu jusqu'à ce qu'on jetât l'éponge en l'air, fallût-il attendre un an. Smiley gagnait toujours avec cette bête-là; malheureusement ils ont fini par dresser un chien qui n'avait pas de pattes de derrière, parce qu'on les avait sciées, et quand les choses furent au point qu'il voulait, et qu'il en vint à se jeter sur son morceau favori, le pauvre chien comprit en un instant qu'on s'était moqué de lui, et que l'autre le tenait. Vous n'avez jamais vu personne avoir l'air plus penaud et plus découragé; il ne fit aucun effort pour gagner le combat et fut rudement secoué, de sorte que, regardant Smiley comme pour lui dire:—Mon cœur est brisé, c'est ta faute; pourquoi m'avoir livré à un chien qui n'a pas de pattes de derrière, puisque c'est par là que je les bats?—il s'en alla en clopinant, et se coucha pour mourir. Ah! c'était un bon chien, cet André Jackson, et il se serait fait un nom, s'il avait vécu, car il y avait de l'etoffe en lui, il avait du génie, je la sais, bien que de grandes occasions lui aient manqué; mais il est impossible de supposer qu'un chien capable de se battre comme lui, certaines circonstances étant données, ait manqué de talent. Je me sens triste toutes les fois que je pense à son dernier combat et au dénoûment qu'il a eu. Eh bien! ce Smiley nourrissait des terriers à rats, et des coqs combat, et des chats, et toute sorte de choses, au point qu'il était toujours en mesure de vous tenir tête, et qu'avec sa rage de paris on n'avait plus de repos. Il attrapa un jour une grenouille et l'emporta chez lui, distant qu'il prétendait faire son éducation; vous me croirez si vous voulez, mais pendant trois mois il n'a rien fait que lui apprendre à sauter dans une cour retirée de sa maison. Et je vous réponds qu'il avait réussi. Il lui donnait un petit coup par derrière, et l'instant d'après vous voyiez la grenouille tourner en l'air comme un beignet au-dessus de la poêle, faire une culbute, quelquefois deux, lorsqu'elle était bien partie, et retomber sur ses pattes comme un chat. Il l'avait dressée dans l'art de gober des mouches, et l'y exerçait continuellement, si bien qu'une mouche, du plus loin qu'elle apparaissait, était une mouche perdue. Smiley avait coutume de dire que tout ce qui manquait à une grenouille, c'était l'éducation, qu'avec l'éducation elle pouvait faire presque tout, et je le crois. Tenez, je l'ai vu poser Daniel Webster là sur se plancher,—Daniel Webster était le nom de la grenouille,—et lui chanter:—Des mouches! Daniel, des mouches!—En un clin d'œil, Daniel avait bondi et saisi une mouche ici sur le comptoir, puis sauté de nouveau par terre, oû il restait vraiment à se gratter la tête avec sa patte de derrière, comme s'il n'avait pas eu la moindre idée de sa supériorité. Jamais vous n'avez grenouille vu de aussi modeste, aussi naturelle, douée comme elle l'était! Et quand il s'agissait de sauter purement et simplement sur terrain plat, elle faisait plus de chemin en un saut qu'aucune bête de son espèce que vous pussiez connaître. Sauter à plat, c'était son fort! Quand il s'agissait de cela, Smiley entassait les enjeux sur elle tant qu'il lui, restait un rouge liard. Il faut le reconnaître, Smiley était monstrueusement fier de sa grenouille, et il en avait le droit, car des gens qui avaient voyagé, qui avaient tout vu, disaient qu'on lui ferait injure de la comparer à une autre; de façon que Smiley gardait Daniel dans une petite boîte à claire-voie qu'il emportait parfois á la ville pour quelque pari.

"Un jour, un individu étranger au camp l'arrête avec sa boîte et lui dit;—Qu'est-ce que vous avez donc serré là dedans?

"Smiley dit d'un air indifférent:—Cela pourrait être un perroquet ou un serin, mais ce n'est rien de pareil, ce n'est qu'une grenouille.

"L'individu la prend, la regarde avec soin, la tourne d'un côté et de l'autre, puis il dit.—Tiens! en effet! A quoi est-elle bonne?

"—Mon Dieu! répond Smiley, toujours d'un air dégagé, elle est bonne pour une chose à mon avis, elle peut battre en sautant toute grenouille du comté de Calaveras.

"L'individu reprend la boîte, l'examine de nouveau longuement, et la rend à Smiley en disant d'un air délibéré:—Eh bien! je ne vois pas que cette grenouille ait rien de mieux qu'aucune grenouille.

"—Possible que vous ne la voyiez pas, dit Smiley, possible que vous vous entendiez en grenouilles, possible que vous ne vous y entendez point, possible que vous ayez de l'expérience, et possible que vous ne soyez qu'un amateur. De toute manière, je parie quarante dollars qu'elle battra en sautant n'importe quelle grenouille du comté de Calaveras.

"L'individu réfléchit une seconde et dit comme attristé:—Je ne suis qu'un étranger ici, je n'ai pas de grenouille; mais, si j'en avais une, je tiendrais le pari.

"—Fort bien! répond Smiley. Rien de plus facile. Si vous ovulez tenir ma boîte une minute, j'irai vous chercher une grenouille.—Voilà donc l'individu qui garde la boîte, qui met ses quarante dollars sur ceux de Smiley et quit attend. Il attend assez longtemps, réfléchissant tout seul, et figurez-vous qu'il prend Daniel, lui ouvre la bouche de force et avec une cuiller à thé l'emplit de menu plomb de chasse, mais l'emplit jusqu'au menton, puis il le pose par terre. Smiley pendant ce temps était à barboter dans une mare. Finalement il attrape une grenouille, l'apporte à cet individu et dit: Maintenant, si vous êtes prêt, mettez-la tout contre Daniel, avec leurs pattes de devant sur la même, ligne, et je donnerai le signal; puis il ajoute:—Un, deux, trois, sautez!

"Lui et l'individu touchent leurs grenouilles par derrière, et la grenouille neuve se met à sautiller, mais Daniel se soulève lourdement, hausse les épaules ainsi, comme un Français; à quoi bon? il ne pouvait bouger, il était planté solide comme une enclume, il n'avançait pas plus que si on l'eût mis à l'ancre. Smiley fut surpris et dégoûté, mais il ne se doutait pas du tour, bien entendu. L'individu empoche l'argent, s'en va, et en s'en allant est-ce qu'il ne donne pas un coup de pouce par-dessus l'épaule, comme ça, au pauvre Daniel, en disant de son air délibéré:—Eh bien! je ne vois pas que cette grenouille ait rien de mieux qu'une autre.

"Smiley se gratta longtemps la tête, les yeux fixés sur Daniel, jusju'à ce qu'enfin il dit:—Je me demande comment diable il se fait que cette bête ait refusé. . . . Est-ce qu'elle aurait quelque chose? . . . On croirait qu'elle est enflée.

"Il empoigne Daniel par la peau du cou, le soulève et dit:—Le loup me croque, s'il ne pèse pas cinq livres.

"Il le retourne, et le malheureux crache deux poignées de plomb. Quand Smiley reconnut ce qui en était, il fut comme fou. Vous le voyez d'ici poser sa grenouille par terre et courir aprés cet individu, mais il ne le rattrapa jamais, et. . . .

THE FROG JUMPING OF THE COUNTY OF CALAVERAS

Translation of the above back from the French.

It there was one time here an individual known under the name of Jim Smiley; it was in the winter of '49, possibly well at the spring of '50, I no me recollect not exactly. This which me makes to believe that it was the one or the other, it is that I shall remember that the grand flume is not achieved when he arrives at the camp for the first time, but of all sides he was the man the most fond of to bet which one have seen, betting upon all that which is presented, when he could find an adversary; and when he not of it could not, he passed to the side opposed. All that which convenienced to the other, to him convenienced also; seeing that he had a bet, Smiley was satisfied. And he had a chance! a chance even worthless; nearly always he gained. It must to say that he was always near to himself expose, but one no could mention the least thing without that this gaillard offered to bet the bottom, no matter what, and to take the side that one him would, as I you it said all at the hour (tout à l'heure). If it there was of races, you him find rich or ruined at the end; if it there is a combat of dogs, he bring his bet; he himself laid always for a combat of cats, for a combat of cocks;—by-blue! If you have see two birds upon a fence, he you should have offered of to bet which of those birds shall fly the first! and if there is *meeting* at the camp (*meeting* au camp) he comes to bet regularly for the curé Walker, which he judged to be the best predicator of the neighborhood (prédicateur des environs), and which he was in effect, and a brave man. He would encounter a bug of wood in the road, whom he will bet upon the time which he shall take to go where she would go—and if you him have take at the word, he will follow the bug as far as Mexique, without himself caring to go so far; neither of the time which he there lost. One time the woman of the curé Walker is very sick during long time, it seemed that one not her saved not; but one morning the curé arrives, and Smiley him demanded how she goes, and he said that she is well better, grace to the infinite misery (lui demande comment elle va, et il dit qu'elle est bien mieux, grâce à l'infinie miséricorde), so much better that with the benediction of the Providence she herself of it would pull out (elle s'en tirerait); and behold that without there thinking Smiley responds: "Well, I gage two-and-half that she will die all of same."

This Smiley had an animal which the boys called the nag of the quarter of hour, but solely for pleasantry, you comprehend, because, well understand, she was more fast as that! [Now why that exclamation?—M. T.] And it was custom of to gain of the silver with this beast, notwithstanding she was poussive, cornarde, always taken of asthma, of colics or of consumption, or something of approaching. One him would give two or three hundred yards at the departure, then one him passed without pain; but never at the last she not fail of herself échauffer, of herself exasperate, and she arrives herself écartant, se défendant, her legs grêles in the air before the obstacles, sometimes them elevating and making with this more of dust than any horse, more of noise above with his éternumens and renitlemens—crac! she arrives then always first by one head, as just as one can it measure. And he had a mall bulldog (bouledogue!) who, to him see, no value, not a cent; one would believe that to bet against him it was to steal, so much he was ordinary; but as soon as the game made, she becomes another dog. Her jaw inferior commence to project like a deck of before, his teeth themselves discover brilliant like some furnaces, and a dog could him tackle (le taquiner), him excite, him murder (le mordre), him throw two or three times over his shoulder, André Jackson—this was the name of the dog—André Jackson takes that tranquilly, as if he not himself was never expecting other thing, and when the bets were doubled and redoubled against him, he you seize the other dog just at the articulation of the leg of behind, and he not it leave more, not that he it masticate, you conceive, but he himself there shall be holding during until that one throws the sponge in the air, must he wait a year. Smiley gained always with this beast-là; unhappily they have finished by elevating a dog who no had not of feet of behind, because one them had sawed; and when things were at the point that he would, and that he came to himself throw upon his morsel favorite, the poor dog comprehended in an instant that he himself was deceived in him, and that the other dog him had. You no have never seen person having the air more penaud and more discouraged; he not made no effort to gain the combat, and was rudely shucked.

Eh bien! this Smiley nourished some terriers à rats, and some cocks of combat, and some cats, and all sorts of things; and with his rage of betting one no had more of repose. He trapped one day a frog and him imported with him (et l'emporta chez lui), saying that he pretended to make his education. You me believe if you will, but during three months he not has nothing done but to him apprehend to jump (apprendre à sauter) in a court retired of her mansion (de sa maison). And I you respond that he have succeeded. He him gives a small blow by behind, and the instant after you shall see the frog turn in the air like a grease-biscuit, make one summersault, sometimes two, when she was well started, and refall upon his feet like a cat. He him had accomplished in the art of to gobble the flies (gober des mouches), and him there exercised continually—so well that a fly at the most far that she appeared was a fly lost. Smiley had custom to say that all which lacked to a frog it was the education, but with the education she could do nearly all—and I him believe. Tenez, I him have seen pose Daniel Webster there upon this plank—Daniel Webster was the name of the frog—and to him sing, "Some flies, Daniel, some flies!"—in a flash of the eye Daniel had bounded and seized a fly here upon the counter, then jumped anew at the earth, where he rested truly to himself scratch the head with his behind foot, as if he no had not the least idea of his superiority. Never you not have seen frog as modest, as natural, sweet as she was. And when he himself agitated to jump purely and simply upon plain earth, she does more ground in one jump than any beast of his species than you can know. To jump plain—this was his strong. When he himself agitated for that, Smiley multiplied the bets upon her as long as there to him remained a red. It must to know, Smiley was monstrously proud of his frog, and he of it was right, for some men who were traveled, who had all seen, said that they to him would be injurious to him compare to another frog. Smiley guarded Daniel in a little box latticed which he carried by-times to the village for some bet.

One day an individual stranger at the camp him arrested with his box and him said:

"What is this that you have them shut up there within?"

Smiley said, with an air indifferent:

"That could be a paroquet, or a syringe (ou un serin), but this no is nothing of such, it not is but a frog."

The individual it took, it regarded with care, it turned from one side and from the other, then he said:

"Tiens! in effect!—At what is she good?"

"My God!" respond Smiley, always with an air disengaged, "she is good for one thing, to my notice (à mon avis), she can batter in jumping (elle peut battre en sautant) all frogs of the county of Calaveras."

The individual retook the box, it examined of new longly, and it rendered to Smiley in saying with an air deliberate:

"Eh bien! I no saw not that that frog had nothing of better than each frog." (Je ne vois pas que cette grenouille ait rien de mieux qu'aucune grenouille.) [If that isn't grammar gone to seed, then I count myself no judge.—M. T.]

"Possible that you not it saw not," said Smiley, "possible that you—you comprehend frogs; possible that you not you there comprehend nothing; possible that you had of the experience, and possible that you not be but an amateur. Of all manner (De toute manière) I bet forty dollars that she batter in jumping no matter which frog of the county of Calaveras."

The individual reflected a second, and said like sad:

"I not am but a stranger here, I no have not a frog; but if I of it had one, I would embrace the bet."

"Strong well!" respond Smiley; "nothing of more facility. If you will hold my box a minute, I go you to search a frog (j'irai vous chercher)."

Behold, then, the individual, who guards the box, who puts his forty dollars upon those of Smiley, and who attends (et qui attend). He attended enough longtimes, reflecting all solely. And figure you that he takes Daniel, him opens the mouth by force and with a teaspoon him fills with shot of the hunt, even him fills just to the chin, then he him puts by the earth. Smiley during these times was at slopping in a swamp. Finally he trapped (attrape) a frog, him carried to that individual, and said:

"Now if you be ready, put him all against Daniel, with their before feet upon the same line, and I give the signal"—then he added: "One, two, three—advance!"

Him and the individual touched their frogs by behind, and the frog new put to jump smartly, but Daniel himself lifted ponderously, exalted the shoulders thus, like a Frenchman—to what good? he not could budge, he is planted solid like a church, he not advance no more than if one him had put at the anchor.

Smiley was surprised and disgusted, but he not himself doubted not of the turn being intended (mais il ne se doutait pas du tour, bien entendu). The individual empocketed the silver, himself with it went, and of it himself in going is it that he no gives not a jerk of thumb over the shoulder—like that—at the poor Daniel, in saying with his air deliberate—(L'individu empoche l'argent, s'en va et en s'en allant est-ce qu'il ne donne pas un coup de pouce par-dessus l'épaule, comme ça, au pauvre Daniel, en disant de son air délibéré):

"Eh bien! *I no see not that that frog has nothing of better than another.*"

Smiley himself scratched longtimes the head, the eyes fixed upon Daniel, until that which at last he said:

"I me demand how the devil it makes itself that this beast has refused. Is it that she had something? One would believe that she is stuffed."

He grasped Daniel by the skin of the neck, him lifted and said:

"The wolf me bite if he no weigh not five pounds."

He him reversed and the unhappy belched two handfuls of shot (et le malheureux, etc.). When Smiley recognized how it was, he was like mad. He deposited his frog by the earth and ran after that individual, but he not him caught never.

Such is the Jumping Frog, to the distorted French eye. I claim that I never put together such an odious mixture of bad grammar and delirium tremens in my life. And what has a poor foreigner like me done, to be abused and misrepresented like this? When I say, "Well, I don't see no p'ints about that frog that's any better'n any other frog," is it kind, is it just, for this Frenchman to try to make it appear that I said, "Eh bien! I no saw not that that frog had nothing of better than each frog"? I have no heart to write more. I never felt so about anything before.

CHAPTER II

THE GLORIOUS WHITEWASHER

SATURDAY morning was come, and all the summer world was bright and fresh, and brimming with life. There was a song in every heart; and if the heart was young the music issued at the lips. There was cheer in every face and a spring in every step. The locust trees were in bloom and the fragrance of the blossoms filled the air. Cardiff Hill, beyond the village and above it, was green with vegetation, and it lay just far enough away to seem a Delectable Land, dreamy, reposeful, and inviting.

Tom appeared on the sidewalk with a bucket of whitewash and a long-handled brush. He surveyed the fence, and all gladness left him and a deep melancholy settled down upon his spirit. Thirty yards of board fence nine feet high. Life to him seemed hollow, and existence but a burden. Sighing he dipped his brush and passed it along the topmost plank; repeated the operation; did it again; compared the insignificant whitewashed streak with the far-reaching continent of unwhitewashed fence, and sat down on a tree-box discouraged. Jim came skipping out at the gate with a tin pail, and singing "Buffalo Gals." Bringing water from the town pump had always been hateful work in Tom's eyes, before, but now it did not strike him so. He remembered that there was company at the pump. White, mulatto, and negro boys and girls were always there waiting their turns, resting, trading playthings, quarreling, fighting, skylarking. And he remembered that although the pump was only a hundred and fifty yards off, Jim never got back with a bucket of water under an hour—and even then somebody generally had to go after him. Tom said:

"Say, Jim, I'll fetch the water if you'll whitewash some."

Jim shook his head and said:

"Can't, Mars Tom. Ole missis, she tole me I got to go an' git dis water an' not stop foolin' roun' wid anybody. She say she spec' Mars Tom gwine to ax me to whitewash, an' so she tole me go 'long an' 'tend to my own business—she 'lowed *she'd* 'tend to de whitewashin'."

"Oh, never you mind what she said, Jim. That's the way she always talks. Gimme the bucket—I won't be gone only a minute. *She* won't ever know."

"Oh, I dasn't, Mars Tom. Ole missis she'd take an' tar de head off'n me. 'Deed she would."

"*She!* She never licks anybody—whacks 'em over the head with her thimble—and who cares for that, I'd like to know. She talks awful, but talk don't hurt—anyways it don't if she don't cry. Jim, I'll give you a marvel. I'll give you a white alley!"

Jim began to waver.

"White alley, Jim! And it's a bully taw."

"My! Dat's a mighty gay marvel, *I* tell you! But Mars Tom I's powerful 'fraid ole missis—"

"And besides, if you will I'll show you my sore toe."

Jim was only human—this attraction was too much for him. He put down his pail, took the white alley, and bent over the toe with absorbing interest while the bandage was being unwound. In another moment he was flying down the street with his pail and a tingling rear, Tom was whitewashing with vigor, and Aunt Polly was retiring from the field with a slipper in her hand and triumph in her eye.

But Tom's energy did not last. He began to think of the fun he had planned for this day, and his sorrows multiplied. Soon the free boys would come tripping along on all sorts of delicious expeditions, and they would make a world of fun of him for having to work—the very thought of it burnt him like fire. He got out his worldly wealth and examined it—bits of toys, marbles, and trash; enough to buy an exchange of *work,* maybe, but not half enough to buy so much as half an hour of pure freedom. So he returned his straitened means to his pocket, and gave up the idea of trying to buy the boys. At this dark and hopeful moment an inspiration burst upon him! Nothing less than a great, magnificent inspiration.

He took up his brush and went tranquilly to work. Ben Rogers hove in sight presently—the very boy, of all boys, whose ridicule he had been dreading. Ben's gait was the hop-skip-and-jump—proof enough that his heart was light and his anticipations high. He was eating an apple, and giving a long, melodious whoop, at intervals, followed by a deep-toned ding-dong-dong, ding-dong-dong, for he was personating a steamboat. As he drew near, he slackened speed, took the middle of the street, leaned far over to starboard and rounded to ponderously and with laborious pomp and circumstance—for he was personating the *Big Missouri,* and considered himself to be drawing nine feet of water. He was boat and captain and engine-bells combined, so he had to imagine himself standing on his own hurricane-deck giving the orders and executing them:

"Stop her, sir! Ting-a-ling-ling!" The headway ran almost out and he drew up slowly toward the sidewalk.

"Ship up to back! Ting-a-ling-ling!" His arms straightened and stiffened down his sides.

"Set her back on the stabboard! Ting-a-ling-ling! Chow! ch-chow-wow! Chow!" His right hand, meantime, describing stately circles—for it was representing a forty-foot wheel.

"Let her go back on the labboard! Ting-a-ling-ling! Chow-ch-chow-chow!" The left hand began to describe circles.

"Stop the stabboard! Ting-a-ling-ling! Stop the labboard! Come ahead on the stabboard! Stop her! Let your outside turn over slow! Ting-a-ling-ling! Chow-ow-ow! Get out that head-line! *Lively* now! Come—out with your spring-line—what 're you about there! Take a turn round that stump with the bight of it! Stand by that stage, now—let her go! Done with the engines,sir! Ting-a-ling-ling! *Sh't! s'h't! sh't!"* (trying the gauge-cocks).

Tom went on whitewashing—paid no attention to the steamboat. Ben stared a moment and then said:

"Hi-*yi! You're* up a stump, ain't you!"

No answer. Tom surveyed his last touch with the eye of an artist, then he gave his brush another gentle sweep and surveyed the result, as before. Ben ranged up alongside of him. Tom's mouth watered for the apple, but he stuck to his work. Ben said:

"Hello, old chap, you got to work, hey?"

Tom wheeled suddenly and said:

"Why, it's you, Ben! I warn't noticing."

"Say—*I*'m going in a-swimming, *I* am. Don't you wish you could? But of course you'd druther *work* — wouldn't you? Course you would!"

Tom contemplated the boy a bit, and said:

"What do you call work?"

"Why, ain't *that* work?"

Tom resumed his whitewashing, and answered carelessly:

"Well, maybe it is, and maybe it ain't. All I know, is, it suits Tom Sawyer."

"Oh come, now, you don't mean to let on that you *like* it?"

The brush continued to move.

"Like it? Well, I don't see why I oughtn't to like it. Does a boy get a chance to whitewash a fence every day?"

That put the thing in a new light. Ben stopped nibbling his apple. Tom swept his brush daintily back and forth—stepped back to note the effect—added a touch here and there—criticized the effect again—Ben watching every move and getting more and more interested, more and more absorbed. Presently he said:

"Say, Tom, let *me* whitewash a little."

Tom considered, was about to consent; but he altered his mind:

"No—no—I reckon it wouldn't hardly do, Ben. You see, Aunt Polly's awful particular about this fence—right here on the street, you know—but if it was the back fence I wouldn't mind and *she* wouldn't. Yes, she's awful particular about this fence; it's got to be done very careful; I reckon there ain't one boy in a thousand, maybe two thousand, that can do it the way it's got to be done."

"No—is that so? Oh come, now—lemme just try. Only just a little—I'd let *you*, if you was me, Tom."

"Ben, I'd like to, honest injun; but Aunt Polly—well, Jim wanted to do it, but she wouldn't let him; Sid wanted to do it, and she wouldn't let Sid. Now don't you see how I'm fixed? If you was to tackle this fence and anything was to happen to it—"

"Oh, shucks, I'll be just as careful. Now lemme try. Say—I'll give you the core of my apple."

"Well, here— No, Ben, now don't. I'm afeard—"

"I'll give you *all* of it!"

Tom gave up the brush with reluctance in his face, but alacrity in his heart. And while the late steamer *Big Missouri* worked and sweated in the sun, the retired artist sat on a barrel in the shade close by, dangled his legs, munched his apple, and planned the slaughter of more innocents. There was no lack of material; boys happened along every little while; they came to jeer, but remained to whitewash. By the time Ben was fagged out, Tom had traded the next chance to Billy Fisher for a kite, in good repair; and when *he* played out, Johnny Miller bought in for a dead rat and a string to swing it with—and so on, and so on, hour after hour. And when the middle of the afternoon came, from being a poor poverty-stricken boy in the morning,

Tom was literally rolling in wealth. He had beside the things before mentioned, twelve marbles, part of a jews-harp, a piece of blue bottle-glass to look through, a spool cannon, a key that wouldn't unlock anything, a fragment of chalk, a glass stopper of a decanter, a tin soldier, a couple of tadpoles, six firecrackers, a kitten with only one eye, a brass door-knob, a dog-collar—but no dog—the handle of a knife, four pieces of orange-peel, and a dilapidated old window-sash.

He had had a nice, good, idle time all the while—plenty of company—and the fence had three coats of whitewash on it! If he hadn't run out of whitewash, he would have bankrupted every boy in the village.

Tom said to himself that it was not such a hollow world, after all. He had discovered a great law of human action, without knowing it—namely, that in order to make a man or a boy covet a thing, it is only necessary to make the thing difficult to attain. If he had been a great and wise philosopher, like the writer of this book, he would now have comprehended that Work consists of whatever a body is *obliged* to do, and that Play consists of whatever a body is not obliged to do. And this would help him to understand why constructing artificial flowers or performing on a treadmill is work, while rolling tenpins or climbing Mont Blanc is only amusement. There are wealthy gentlemen in England who drive four-horse passenger-coaches twenty or thirty miles on a daily line, in the summer, because the privilege costs them considerable money; but if they were offered wages for the service, that would turn it into work and then they would resign.

The boy mused awhile over the substantial change which had taken place in his worldly circumstances, and then wended toward headquarters to report.

ON THE DECAY OF THE ART OF LYING

From Tom Sawyer Abroad, Tom Sawyer Detective and Other Stories

Essay, for discussion, read at a meeting of the Historical and Antiquarian Club of Hartford, and offered for the thirty-dollar prize. Now first published.[1]

Observe, I do not mean to suggest that the *custom* of lying has suffered any decay or interruption—no, for the Lie, as a Virtue, a Principle, is eternal; the Lie, as a recreation, a solace, a refuge in time of need, the fourth Grace, the tenth Muse, man's best and surest friend, is immortal, and cannot perish from the earth while this Club remains. My complaint simply concerns the decay of the *art* of lying. No high-minded man, no man of right feeling, can contemplate the lumbering and slovenly lying of the present day without grieving to see a noble art so prostituted. In this veteran presence I naturally enter upon this scheme with diffidence; it is like an old maid trying to teach nursery matters to the mothers in Israel. It would not become me to criticize you, gentlemen, who are nearly all my elders—and my superiors, in this thing—and so, if I should here and there *seem* to do it, I trust it will in most cases be more in a spirit of admiration than of fault-finding; indeed, if this finest of the fine arts had everywhere received the attention, encouragement, and conscientious practice and development which this Club has devoted to it, I should not need to utter this lament or shed a single tear. I do not say this to flatter: I say it in a spirit of just and appreciative recognition.

[It had been my intention, at this point, to mention names and give illustrative specimens, but indications observable about me admonished me to beware of particulars and confine myself to generalities.]

No fact is more firmly established than that lying is a necessity of our circumstances—the deduction that it is then a Virtue goes without saying. No virtue can reach its highest usefulness without careful and diligent cultivation—therefore, it goes without saying that this one ought to be taught in the public schools

[1] Did not take the prize.—M. T.

—at the fireside—even in the newspapers. What chance has the ignorant, uncultivated liar against the educated expert? What chance have I against Mr. Per—against a lawyer? *Judicious* lying is what the world needs. I sometimes think it were even better and safer not to lie at all than to lie injudiciously. An awkward, unscientific lie is often as ineffectual as the truth.

Now let us see what the philosophers say. Note that venerable proverb: Children and fools *always* speak the truth. The deduction is plain—adults and wise persons never speak it. Parkman, the historian, says, "The principle of truth may itself be carried into an absurdity." In another place in the same chapter he says, "The saying is old that truth should not be spoken at all times; and those whom a sick conscience worries into habitual violation of the maxim are imbeciles and nuisances." It is strong language, but true. None of us could *live* with an habitual truth-teller; but, thank goodness, none of us has to. An habitual truth-teller is simply an impossible creature; he does not exist; he never has existed. Of course there are people who *think* they never lie, but it is not so—and this ignorance is one of the very things that shame our so-called civilization. Everybody lies—every day; every hour; awake; asleep; in his dreams; in his joy; in his mourning; if he keeps his tongue still, his hands, his feet, his eyes, his attitude, will convey deception—and purposely. Even in sermons—but that is a platitude.

In a far country where I once lived the ladies used to go around paying calls, under the humane and kindly pretense of wanting to see each other; and when they returned home, they would cry out with a glad voice, saying, "We made sixteen calls and found fourteen of them out"—not meaning that they found out anything against the fourteen—no, that was only a colloquial phrase to signify that they were not at home—and their manner of saying it expressed their lively satisfaction in that fact. Now their pretense of wanting to see the fourteen—and the other two whom they had been less lucky with—was that commonest and mildest form of lying which is sufficiently described as a deflection from the truth. Is it justifiable? Most certainly. It is beautiful, it is noble; for its object is, *not* to reap profit, but to convey a pleasure to the sixteen. The iron-souled truth-monger would plainly manifest, or even utter the fact, that he didn't want to see those people—and he would be an ass, and inflict a totally unnecessary pain. And next, those ladies in that far country—but never mind, they had a thousand pleasant ways of lying, that grew out of gentle impulses, and were a credit to their intelligence and an honor to their hearts. Let the particulars go.

The men in that far country were liars, every one. Their mere howdy-do was a lie, because *they* didn't care how you did, except they were undertakers. To the ordinary inquirer you lied in return; for you made no conscientious diagnosis of your case, but answered at random, and usually missed it considerably. You lied to the undertaker, and said your health was failing—a wholly commendable lie, since it cost you nothing and pleased the other man. If a stranger called and interrupted you, you said with your hearty tongue, "I'm glad to see you," and said with your heartier soul, "I wish you were with the cannibals and it was dinner-time." When he went, you said regretfully, "*Must* you go?" and followed it with a "Call again"; but you did no harm, for you did not deceive anybody nor inflict any hurt, whereas the truth would have made you both unhappy.

I think that all this courteous lying is a sweet and loving art, and should be cultivated. The highest perfection of politeness is only a beautiful edifice, built, from the base to the dome, of graceful and gilded forms of charitable and unselfish lying.

What I bemoan is the growing prevalence of the brutal truth. Let us do what we can to eradicate it. An injurious truth has no merit over an injurious lie. Neither should ever be uttered. The man who speaks an injurious truth, lest his soul be not saved if he do otherwise, should reflect that that sort of a soul is not strictly worth saving. The man who tells a lie to help a poor devil out of trouble is one of whom the angels doubtless say, "Lo, here is an heroic soul who casts his own welfare into jeopardy to succor his neighbor's; let us exalt this magnanimous liar."

An injurious lie is an uncommendable thing; and so, also, and in the same degree, is an injurious truth—a fact which is recognized by the law of libel.

Among other common lies, we have the *silent* lie—the deception which one conveys by simply keeping still and concealing the truth. Many obstinate truth-mongers indulge in this dissipation, imagining that if they *speak* no lie, they lie not at all. In that far country where I once lived, there was a lovely spirit, a lady whose impulses were always high and pure, and whose character answered to them. One day I was there at dinner, and remarked, in a general way, that we are all liars. She was amazed, and said, "Not *all?*" It was before *Pinafore's*[1] time, so I did not make the response which would naturally follow in our day, but frankly said, "Yes, *all*—we are all liars; there are no exceptions." She looked almost offended, and said, "Why, do you include *me?*" Certainly," I said, "I think you even rank as an expert." She said, " 'Sh!—'sh! the children!" So the subject was changed in deference to the children's presence, and we went on talking about other things. But as soon as the young people were out of the way, the lady came warmly back to the matter and said, "I have made it the rule of my life to never tell a lie; and I have never departed from it in a single instance." I said, "I don't mean the least harm or disrespect, but really you have been lying like smoke ever since I've been sitting here. It has caused me a good deal of pain, because I am not used to it." She required of me an instance—just a single instance. So I said:

"Well, here is the unfilled duplicate of the blank which the Oakland hospital people sent to you by the hand of the sick-nurse when she came here to nurse your little nephew through his dangerous illness. This blank asks all manner of questions as to the conduct of that sick-nurse: 'Did she ever sleep on her watch? Did she ever forget to give the medicine?' and so forth and so on. You are warned to be very careful and explicit in your answers, for the welfare of the service requires that the nurses be promptly fined or otherwise punished for derelictions. You told me you were perfectly delighted with that nurse—that she had a thousand perfections and only one fault: you found you never could depend on her wrapping Johnny up half sufficiently while he waited in a chilly chair for her to rearrange the warm bed. You filled up the duplicate of this paper, and sent it back to the hospital by the hand of the nurse. How did you answer this question—'Was the nurse at any time guilty of a negligence which was likely to result in the patient's taking cold?' Come—everything is decided by a bet here in California: ten dollars to ten cents you lied when you answered that question." She said, "I didn't; *I left it blank!*" "Just so—you have told a *silent* lie; you have left it to be inferred that you had no fault to find in that matter." She said, "Oh, was that a lie? And how *could* I mention her one single fault, and she so good? —it would have been cruel." I said, "One ought always to lie

[1]The famous opera of Gilbert and Sullivan. Mark Twain is probably thinking of the passage in which the captain asserts he never swears. The bystanders inquire, "What, *never?*" and he rejoins; "Well—hardly ever."

when one can do good by it; your impulse was right, but your judgment was crude; this comes of unintelligent practice. Now observe the result of this inexpert deflection of yours. You know Mr. Jones's Willie is lying very low with scarlet fever; well, your recommendation was so enthusiastic that that girl is there nursing him, and the worn-out family have all been trustingly sound asleep for the last fourteen hours, leaving their darling with full confidence in those fatal hands, because you, like young George Washington, have a reputa— However, if you are not going to have anything to do, I will come around tomorrow and we'll attend the funeral together, for, of course, you'll naturally feel a peculiar interest in Willie's case—as personal a one, in fact, as the undertaker."

But that was all lost. Before I was half-way through she was in a carriage and making thirty miles an hour toward the Jones mansion to save what was left of Willie and tell all she knew about the deadly nurse. All of which was unnecessary, as Willie wasn't sick; I had been lying myself. But that same day, all the same, she sent a line to the hospital which filled up the neglected blank, and stated the *facts,* too, in the squarest possible manner.

Now, you see, this lady's fault was *not* in lying, but only in lying injudiciously. She should have told the truth, *there,* and made it up to the nurse with a fraudulent compliment further along in the paper. She could have said, "In one respect the sick-nurse is perfection—when she is on watch, she never snores." Almost any little pleasant lie would have taken the sting out of that troublesome but necessary expression of the truth.

Lying is universal—we *all* do it; we all *must* do it. Therefore, the wise thing is for us diligently to train ourselves to lie thoughtfully, judiciously; to lie with a good object, and not an evil one; to lie for others' advantage, and not our own; to lie healingly, charitably, humanely, not cruelly, hurtfully, maliciously; to lie gracefully and graciously, not awkwardly and clumsily; to lie firmly, frankly, squarely, with head erect, not haltingly, tortuously, with pusillanimous mien, as being ashamed of our high calling. Then shall we be rid of the rank and pestilent truth that is rotting the land; then shall we be great and good and beautiful, and worthy dwellers in a world where even benign Nature habitually lies, except when she promises execrable weather. Then— But I am but a new and feeble student in this gracious art; I cannot instruct *this* Club.

Joking aside, I think there is much need of wise examination into what sorts of lies are best and wholesomest to be indulged, seeing we *must* all lie and *do* all lie, and what sorts it may be best to avoid—and this is a thing which I feel I can confidently put into the hands of this experienced Club—a ripe body, who may be termed, in this regard, and without undue flattery, Old Masters.

PUNCH, BROTHERS, PUNCH

From Tom Sawyer Abroad, Tom Sawyer Detective and Other Stories

Will the reader please to cast his eye over the following lines, and see if he can discover anything harmful in them?

> Conductor, when you receive a fare,
> Punch in the presence of the passenjare!
> A blue trip slip for an eight-cent fare,
> A buff trip slip for a six-cent fare,
> A pink trip slip for a three-cent fare,
> Punch in the presence of the passenjare!
>
> CHORUS
>
> Punch, brothers! punch with care!
> Punch in the presence of the passenjare!

I came across these jingling rhymes in a newspaper, a little while ago, and read them a couple of times. They took instant and entire possession of me. All through breakfast they went waltzing through my brain; and when, at last, I rolled up my napkin, I could not tell whether I had eaten anything or not. I had carefully laid out my day's work the day before — a thrilling tragedy in the novel which I am writing. I went to my den to begin my deed of blood. I took up my pen, but all I could get it to say was, "Punch in the presence of the passenjare." I fought hard for an hour, but it was useless. My head kept humming, "A blue trip slip for an eight-cent fare, a buff trip slip for a six-cent fare," and so on and so on, without peace or respite. The day's work was ruined—I could see that plainly enough. I gave up and drifted down-town, and presently discovered that my feet were keeping time to that relentless jingle. When I could stand it no longer I altered my step. But it did no good; those rhymes accommodated themselves to the new step and went on harassing me just as before. I returned home, and suffered all the afternoon; suffered all through an unconscious and unrefreshing dinner; suffered, and cried, and jingled all through the evening; went to bed and rolled, tossed, and jingled right along, the same as ever; got up at midnight frantic, and tried to read; but there was nothing visible upon the whirling page except "Punch! punch in the presence of the passenjare." By sunrise I was out of my mind, and everybody marveled and was distressed at the idiotic burden of my ravings—"Punch! oh, punch! punch in the presence of the passenjare!"

Two days later, on Saturday morning, I arose, a tottering wreck, and went forth to fulfil an engagement with a valued friend, the Rev. Mr. ———, to walk to the Talcott Tower, ten miles distant. He stared at me, but asked no questions. We started. Mr. ——— talked, talked, talked—as is his wont. I said nothing; I heard nothing. At the end of a mile, Mr. ——— said:

"Mark, are you sick? I never saw a man look so haggard and worn and absent-minded. Say something, do!"

Drearily, without enthusiasm, I said: "Punch, brothers, punch with care! Punch in the presence of the passenjare!"

My friend eyed me blankly, looked perplexed, then said:

"I do not think I get your drift, Mark. There does not seem to be any relevancy in what you have said, certainly nothing sad; and yet—maybe it was the way you *said* the words—I never heard anything that sounded so pathetic. What is ———"

But I heard no more. I was already far away with my pitiless, heartbreaking "blue trip slip for an eight-cent fare, buff trip slip for a six-cent fare, pink trip slip for a three-cent fare; punch in the presence of the passenjare." I do not know what occurred during the other nine miles. However, all of a sudden Mr. ——— laid his hand on my shoulder and shouted:

"Oh, wake up! wake up! wake up! Don't sleep all day! Here we are at the Tower, man! I have talked myself deaf and dumb and blind, and never got a response. Just look at this magnificent autumn landscape! Look at it! look at it! Feast your eyes on it! You have traveled; you have seen boasted landscapes elsewhere. Come, now, deliver an honest opinion. What do you say to this?"

I sighed wearily, and murmured:

"A buff trip slip for a six-cent fare, a pink trip slip for a three-cent fare, punch in the presence of the passenjare."

Rev. Mr. ——— stood there, very grave, full of concern, apparently, and looked long at me; then he said:

"Mark, there is something about this that I cannot understand. Those are about the same words you said before; there does not seem to be anything in them, and yet they nearly break my heart when you say them. Punch in the—how is it they go?"

I began at the beginning and repeated all the lines.

My friend's face lighted with interest. He said:

"Why, what a captivating jingle it is! It is almost music. It flows along so nicely. I have nearly caught the rhymes myself. Say them over just once more, and then I'll have them, sure."

I said them over. Then Mr. ——— said them. He made one little mistake, which I corrected. The next time and the next he got them right. Now a great burden seemed to tumble from my shoulders. That torturing jingle departed out of my brain, and a grateful sense of rest and peace descended upon me. I was light-hearted enough to sing; and I did sing for half an hour, straight along, as we went jogging homeward. Then my freed tongue found blessed speech again, and the pent talk of many a weary hour began to gush and flow. It flowed on and on, joyously, jubilantly, until the fountain was empty and dry. As I wrung my friend's hand at parting, I said:

"Haven't we had a royal good time! But now I remember, you haven't said a word for two hours. Come, come, out with something!"

The Rev. Mr. ——— turned a lack-luster eye upon me, drew a deep sigh, and said, without animation, without apparent consciousness:

"Punch, brothers, punch with care! Punch in the presence of the passenjare!"

A pang shot through me as I said to myself, "Poor fellow, poor fellow! *he* has got it now."

I did not see Mr. ——— for two or three days after that. Then, on Tuesday evening, he staggered into my presence and sank dejectedly into a seat. He was pale, worn; he was a wreck. He lifted his faded eyes to my face and said:

"Ah, Mark, it was a ruinous investment that I made in those heartless rhymes. They have ridden me like a nightmare, day and night, hour after hour, to this very moment. Since I saw you I have suffered the torments of the lost. Saturday evening I had a sudden call, by telegraph, and took the night train for Boston. The occasion was the death of a valued old friend who had requested that I should preach his funeral sermon. I took my seat in the cars and set myself to framing the discourse. But I never got beyond the opening paragraph; for then the train started and the car-wheels began their 'clack, clack—clack-clack-clack! clack-clack — clack-clack-clack!' and right away those odious rhymes fitted themselves to that accompaniment. For an hour I sat there and set a syllable of those rhymes to every separate and distinct clack the car-wheels made. Why, I was as fagged out, then, as if I had been chopping wood all day. My skull was splitting with headache. It seemed to me that I must go mad if I sat there any longer; so I undressed and went to bed. I stretched myself out in my berth, and—well, you know what the result was. The thing went right along, just the same. 'Clack-clack-clack, a blue trip slip, clack-clack-clack, for an eight-cent fare; clack-clack-clack, a buff trip slip, clack-clack-clack, for a six-cent fare, and so on, and so on, and so on—*punch* in the presence of the passenjare!' Sleep? Not a single wink! I was almost a lunatic when I got to Boston. Don't ask me about the funeral. I did the best I could, but every solemn individual sentence was meshed and tangled and woven in and out with 'Punch, brothers, punch with care, punch in the presence of the passenjare.' And the most distressing thing was that my delivery dropped into the undulating rhythm of those pulsing rhymes, and I could actually catch absent-minded people nodding *time* to the swing of it with their stupid heads. And, Mark, you may believe it or not, but before I got through the entire assemblage were placidly bobbing their heads in solemn unison, mourners, undertaker, and all. The moment I had finished, I fled to the anteroom in a state bordering on frenzy. Of course it would be my luck to find a sorrowing and aged maiden aunt of the deceased there, who had arrived from Springfield too late to get into the church. She began to sob, and said:

"'Oh, oh, he is gone, he is gone, and I didn't see him before he died!'

"'Yes!' I said, 'he *is* gone, he *is* gone, he *is* gone—oh, *will* this suffering never cease!'

"'You loved him, then! Oh, you too loved him!'

"'Loved him! Loved *who?*'

"'Why, my poor George! my poor nephew!'

"'Oh—*him!* Yes—oh, yes, yes. Certainly—certainly. Punch—punch—oh, this misery will kill me!'

"'Bless you! bless you, sir, for these sweet words! *I*, too, suffer in this dear loss. Were you present during his last moments?'

"'Yes. I—*whose* last moments?'

"'*His*. The dear departed's.'

"'Yes! Oh, yes—yes—*yes!* I suppose so, I think so, *I* don't know! Oh, certainly—I was there—*I* was there!'

"'Oh, what a privilege! what a precious privilege! And his last words—oh, tell me, tell me his last words! What did he say?'

"'He said—he said—oh, my head, my head, my head! He said—he said—he never said *any*thing but Punch, punch, ***punch*** in the presence of the passenjare! Oh, leave me, madam! In the name of all that is generous, leave me to my madness, my misery, my despair!—a buff trip slip for a six-cent fare, a pink trip slip for a three-cent fare—endu-rance *can* no fur-ther go!—PUNCH in the presence of the passenjare!'"

My friend's hopeless eyes rested upon mine a pregnant minute, and then he said impressively:

"Mark, you do not say anything. You do not offer me any hope. But, ah me, it is just as well—it is just as well. You could not do me any good. The time has long gone by when words could comfort me. Something tells me that my tongue is doomed to wag forever to the jigger of that remorseless jingle. There—there it is coming on me again: a blue trip slip for an eight-cent fare, a buff trip slip for a ——"

Thus murmuring faint and fainter, my friend sank into a peaceful trance and forgot his sufferings in a blessed respite.

How did I finally save him from an asylum? I took him to a neighboring university and made him discharge the burden of his persecuting rhymes into the eager ears of the poor, unthinking students. How is it with *them,* now? The result is too sad to tell. Why did I write this article? It was for a worthy, even a noble, purpose. It was to warn you, reader, if you should come across those merciless rhymes, to avoid them—avoid them as you would a pestilence!

THE DEATH OF JEAN

From WHAT IS MAN? AND OTHER ESSAYS

The death of Jean Clemens occurred early in the morning of December 24, 1909. Mr. Clemens was in great stress of mind when I first saw him, but a few hours later I found him writing steadily.

"I am setting it down," he said, "everything It is a relief to me to write it. It furnishes me an excuse for thinking." At intervals during that day and the next I looked in, and usually found him writing. Then on the evening of the 26th, when he knew that Jean had been laid to rest in Elmira, he came to my room with the manuscript in his hand.

"I have finished it," he said; "read it. I can form no opinion of it myself. If you think it worthy, some day—at the proper time—it can end my autobiography. It is the final chapter."

Four months later—almost to the day—(April 21st) he was with Jean.—ALBERT BIGELOW PAINE.

Stormfield, Christmas Eve, 11 A.M., 1909

JEAN is dead!

Has any one ever tried to put upon paper all the little happenings connected with a dear one—happenings of the twenty-four hours preceding the sudden and unexpected death of that dear one? Would a book contain them? Would two books contain them? I think not. They pour into the mind in a flood. They are little things that have been always happening every day, and were always so unimportant and easily forgettable before—but now! Now, how different! how precious they are, how dear, how unforgettable, how pathetic, how sacred, how clothed with dignity!

Last night Jean, all flushed with splendid health, and I the same from the wholesome effects of my Bermuda holiday, strolled hand in hand from the dinner-table and sat down in the library and chatted, and planned, and discussed, cheerily and happily (and how unsuspectingly!)—until nine—which is late for us—then went upstairs, Jean's friendly German dog following. At my door Jean said, "I can't kiss you good night, father: I have a cold, and you could catch it." I bent and kissed her hand She was moved—I saw it in her eyes—and she impulsively kissed my hand in return. Then with the usual gay "Sleep well, dear!" from both, we parted.

At half past seven this morning I woke, and heard voices outside my door. I said to myself, "Jean is starting on her usual horseback flight to the station for the mail." Then Katy[1] entered, stood quaking and gasping at my bedside a moment, then found her tongue:

"Miss Jean is dead!"

Possibly I know now what the soldier feels when a bullet crashes through his heart.

In her bathroom there she lay, the fair young creature, stretched upon the floor and covered with a sheet. And looking so placid, so natural, and as if asleep. We knew what had happened. She was an epileptic: she had been seized with a convulsion and heart failure in her bath. The doctor had to come several miles. His efforts, like our previous ones, failed to bring her back to life.

It is noon, now. How lovable she looks, how sweet and how tranquil! It is a noble face, and full of dignity; and that was a good heart that lies there so still.

In England, thirteen years ago, my wife and I were stabbed to the heart with a cablegram which said, "Susy was mercifully released to-day." I had to send a like shock to Clara, in Berlin, this morning. With the peremptory addition, "You must not come home." Clara and her husband sailed from here on the 11th of this month. How will Clara bear it? Jean, from her babyhood, was a worshiper of Clara.

Four days ago I came back from a month's holiday in Bermuda in perfected health; but by some accident the reporters failed to perceive this. Day before yesterday, letters and telegrams began to arrive from friends and strangers which indicated that I was supposed to be dangerously ill. Yesterday Jean begged me to explain my case through the Associated Press. I said it was not important enough; but she was distressed and said I must think of Clara. Clara would see the report in the German papers, and as she had been nursing her husband day and night for four months[2] and was worn out and feeble, the shock might be disastrous. There was reason in that; so I sent a humorous paragraph by telephone to the Associated Press denying the "charge" that I was "dying," and saying "I

[1]Katy Leary, who had been in the service of the Clemens family for twenty-nine years.

[2]Mr. Gabrilowitsch had been operated on for appendicitis.

would not do such a thing at my time of life."

Jean was a little troubled, and did not like to see me treat the matter so lightly; but I said it was best to treat it so, for there was nothing serious about it. This morning I sent the sorrowful facts of this day's irremediable disaster to the Associated Press. Will both appear in this evening's papers?—the one so blithe, the other so tragic.

I lost Susy thirteen years ago; I lost her mother—her incomparable mother!—five and a half years ago; Clara has gone away to live in Europe; and now I have lost Jean. How poor I am, who was once so rich! Seven months ago Mr. Rogers died—one of the best friends I ever had, and the nearest perfect, as man and gentleman, I have yet met among my race; within the last six weeks Gilder has passed away, and Laffan—old, old friends of mine. Jean lies yonder, I sit here; we are strangers under our own roof; we kissed hands good-bye at this door last night—and it was forever, we never suspecting it. She lies there, and I sit here—writing, busying myself, to keep my heart from breaking. How dazzlingly the sunshine is flooding the hills around! It is like a mockery.

Seventy-four years old twenty-four days ago. Seventy-four years old yesterday. Who can estimate my age to-day?

I have looked upon her again. I wonder I can bear it. She looks just as her mother looked when she lay dead in that Florentine villa so long ago. The sweet placidity of death! it is more beautiful than sleep.

I saw her mother buried. I said I would never endure that horror again; that I would never again look into the grave of any one dear to me. I have kept to that. They will take Jean from this house to-morrow, and bear her to Elmira, New York, where lie those of us that have been released, but I shall not follow.

Jean was on the dock when the ship came in, only four days ago. She was at the door, beaming a welcome, when I reached this house the next evening. We played cards, and she tried to teach me a new game called "Mark Twain." We sat chatting cheerily in the library last night, and she wouldn't let me look into the loggia, where she was making Christmas preparations. She said she would finish them in the morning, and then her little French friend would arrive from New York—the surprise would follow; the surprise she had been working over for days. While she was out for a moment I disloyally stole a look. The loggia floor was clothed with rugs and furnished with chairs and sofas; and the uncompleted surprise was there: in the form of a Christmas tree that was drenched with silver film in a most wonderful way; and on a table was a prodigal profusion of bright things which she was going to hang upon it to-day. What desecrating hand will ever banish that eloquent unfinished surprise from that place? Not mine, surely. All these little matters have happened in the last four days. "Little." Yes—*then.* But not now. Nothing she said or thought or did is little now. And all the lavish humor!—what is become of it? It is pathos, now. Pathos, and the thought of it brings tears.

All these little things happened such a few hours ago—and now she lies yonder. Lies yonder, and cares for nothing any more. Strange—marvelous—incredible! I have had this experience before; but it would still be incredible if I had had it a thousand times.

"Miss Jean is dead!"

That is what Katy said. When I heard the door open behind the bed's head without a preliminary knock, I supposed it was Jean coming to kiss me good morning, she being the only person who was used to entering without formalities.

And so ——

I have been to Jean's parlor. Such a turmoil of Christmas presents for servants and friends! They are everywhere; tables, chairs, sofas, the floor—everything is occupied, and over-occupied. It is many and many a year since I have seen the like. In that ancient day Mrs. Clemens and I used to slip softly into the nursery at midnight on Christmas Eve and look the array of presents over. The children were little then. And now here is Jean's parlor looking just as that nursery used to look. The presents are not labeled—the hands are forever idle that would have labeled them to-day. Jean's mother always worked herself down with her Christmas preparations. Jean did the same yesterday and the preceding days, and the fatigue has cost her her life. The fatigue caused the convulsion that attacked her this morning. She had had no attack for months.

Jean was so full of life and energy that she was constantly in danger of overtaxing her strength. Every morning she was in the saddle by half past seven, and off to the station for her mail. She examined the letters and I distributed them: some to her, some to Mr. Paine, the others to the stenographer and myself. She despatched her share and then mounted her horse again and went around superintending her farm and her poultry the rest of the day. Sometimes she played billiards with me after dinner, but she was usually too tired to play, and went early to bed.

Yesterday afternoon I told her about some plans I had been devising while absent in Bermuda, to lighten her burdens. We would get a housekeeper; also we would put her share of the secretary-work into Mr. Paine's hands.

No—she wasn't willing. She had been making plans herself. The matter ended in a compromise. I submitted. I always did. She wouldn't audit the bills and let Paine fill out the checks—she would continue to attend to that herself. Also, she would continue to be housekeeper, and let Katy assist. Also, she would continue to answer the letters of personal friends for me. Such was the compromise. Both of us called it by that name, though I was not able to see where any formidable change had been made.

However, Jean was pleased, and that was sufficient for me. She was proud of being my secretary, and I was never able to persuade her to give up any part of her share in that unlovely work.

In the talk last night I said I found everything going so smoothly that if she were willing I would go back to Bermuda in February and get blessedly out of the clash and turmoil again for another month. She was urgent that I should do it, and said that if I would put off the trip until March she would take Katy and go with me. We struck hands upon that, and said it was settled. I had a mind to write to Bermuda by to-morrow's ship and secure a furnished house and servants. I meant to write the letter this morning. But it will never be written, now.

For she lies yonder, and before her is another journey than that.

Night is closing down; the rim of the sun barely shows above the sky-line of the hills.

I have been looking at that face again that was growing dearer and dearer to me every day. I was getting acquainted with Jean in these last nine months. She had been long an exile from home when she came to us three-quarters of a year ago. She had been shut up in sanitariums, many miles from us. How eloquently glad and grateful she was to cross her father's threshold again!

Would I bring her back to life if I could do it? I would not. If a word would do it, I would beg for strength to withhold the word. And I would have the strength; I am sure of it. In her loss I am almost bankrupt, and my life is a bitterness, but I am content: for she has been enriched with the most precious of all gifts—that gift which makes all other gifts mean and poor—death. I have never wanted any released friend of mine restored to life since I reached manhood. I felt in this way when Susy passed away; and later my wife, and later Mr. Rogers. When Clara met me at the station in New York and told me Mr. Rogers had died suddenly that morning, my thought was, Oh, favorite of fortune—fortunate all his long and lovely life—fortunate to his latest moment! The reporters said there were tears of sorrow in my eyes. True—but they were for *me*, not for him. He had suffered no loss. All the fortunes he had ever made before were poverty compared with this one.

Why did I build this house, two years ago? To shelter this vast emptiness? How foolish I was! But I shall stay in it. The spirits of the dead hallow a house, for me. It was not so with other members of my family. Susy died in the house we built in Hartford. Mrs. Clemens would never enter it again. But it made the house dearer to me. I have entered it once since, when it was tenantless and silent and forlorn, but to me it was a holy place and beautiful. It seemed to me that the spirits of the dead were all about me, and would speak to me and welcome me if they could: Livy, and Susy, and George, and Henry Robinson, and Charles Dudley Warner. How good and kind they were, and how lovable their lives! In fancy I could see them all again, I could call the children back and hear them romp again with George—that peerless black ex-slave and children's idol who came one day—a flitting stranger—to wash windows, and stayed eighteen years. Until he died. Clara and Jean would never enter again the New York hotel which their mother had frequented in earlier days. They could not bear it. But I shall stay in this house. It is dearer to me to-night than ever it was before. Jean's spirit will make it beautiful for me always. Her lonely and tragic death—but I will not think of that now.

Jean's mother always devoted two or three weeks to Christmas shopping, and was always physically exhausted when Christmas Eve came. Jean was her very own child—she wore herself out present-hunting in New York these latter days. Paine has just found on her desk a long list of names—fifty, he thinks—people to whom she sent presents last night. Apparently she forgot no one. And Katy found there a roll of bank-notes, for the servants.

Her dog has been wandering about the grounds to-day, comradeless and forlorn. I have seen him from the windows. She got him from Germany. He has tall ears and looks exactly like a wolf. He was educated in Germany, and knows no language but the German. Jean gave him no orders save in that tongue. And so, when the burglar-alarm made a fierce clamor at midnight a fortnight ago, the butler, who is French and knows no German, tried in vain to interest the dog in the supposed burglar. Jean wrote me, to Bermuda, about the incident. It was the last letter I was ever to receive from her bright head and her competent hand. The dog will not be neglected.

There was never a kinder heart than Jean's. From her childhood up she always spent the most of her allowance on charities of one kind and another. After she became secretary and had her income doubled she spent her money upon these things with a free hand. Mine too, I am glad and grateful to say.

She was a loyal friend to all animals, and she loved them all, birds, beasts, and everything—even snakes—an inheritance from me. She knew all the birds: she was high up in that lore. She became a member of various humane societies when she was still a little girl—both here and abroad—and she remained an active member to the last. She founded two or three societies for the protection of animals, here and in Europe.

She was an embarrassing secretary, for she fished my correspondence out of the waste-basket and answered the letters. She thought all letters deserved the courtesy of an answer. Her mother brought her up in that kindly error.

She could write a good letter, and was swift with her pen. She had but an indifferent ear for music, but her tongue took to languages with an easy facility. She never allowed her Italian, French, and German to get rusty through neglect.

The telegrams of sympathy are flowing in, from far and wide, now, just as they did in Italy five years and a half ago, when this child's mother laid down her blameless life. They cannot heal the hurt, but they take away some of the pain. When Jean and I kissed hands and parted at my door last, how little did we imagine that in twenty-two hours the telegraph would be bringing words like these:

"From the bottom of our hearts we send our sympathy, dearest of friends."

For many and many a day to come, wherever I go in this house, remembrances of Jean will mutely speak to me of her. Who can count the number of them?

She was in exile two years with the hope of healing her malady—epilepsy. There are no words to express how grateful I am that she did not meet her fate in the hands of strangers, but in the loving shelter of her own home.

"Miss Jean is dead!"

It is true. Jean is dead.

A month ago I was writing bubbling and hilarious articles for magazines yet to appear, and now I am writing—this.

Christmas Day. Noon.—Last night I went to Jean's room at intervals, and turned back the sheet and looked at the peaceful face, and kissed the cold brow, and remembered that heart-breaking night in Florence so long ago, in that cavernous and silent vast villa, when I crept down-stairs so many times, and turned back a sheet and looked at a face just like this one—Jean's mother's face—and kissed a brow that was just like this one. And last night I saw again what I had seen then—that strange and lovely miracle—the sweet, soft contours of early maidenhood restored by the gracious hand of death! When Jean's mother lay dead, all trace of care, and trouble, and suffering, and the corroding years had vanished out of the face, and I was looking again upon it as I had known and worshiped it in its young bloom and beauty a whole generation before.

About three in the morning, while wandering about the house in the deep silences, as one does in times like these, when there is a dumb sense that something has been lost that will never be found again, yet must be sought, if only for the employment the useless seeking gives, I came upon Jean's dog in the hall down-stairs, and noted that he did not spring to greet me, according to his hospitable habit, but came slow and sorrowfully; also I remembered that he had not visited Jean's apartment since the tragedy. Poor fellow, did he know? I think so. Always when Jean was abroad in the open he was with her; always when she was in the house he was with her, in the night as well as in the day. Her parlor was his bedroom. Whenever I happened upon him on the ground floor he always followed me about, and when I went up-stairs he went too—in a tumultuous gallop. But now it was different: after patting him a little I went to the library—he remained behind: when I went up-stairs he did not follow me, save with his wistful eyes. He has wonderful eyes—big, and kind, and eloquent. He can talk with them. He is a beautiful creature, and is of the breed of the New York police-dogs. I do not like dogs, because they bark when there is no occasion for it; but I have liked this one from the beginning, because he belonged to Jean, and because he never barks except when there is occasion—which is not oftener than twice a week.

In my wanderings I visited Jean's parlor. On a shelf I found a pile of my books, and I knew what it meant. She was waiting for me to come home from Bermuda and autograph them, then she would send them away. If I only knew whom she intended them for! But I shall never know. I will keep them. Her hand has touched them—it is an accolade—they are noble, now.

And in a closet she had hidden a surprise for me—a thing I have often wished I owned: a noble big globe. I couldn't see it for the tears. She will never know the pride I take in it, and the pleasure. To-day the mails are full of loving remembrances for her: full of those old, old kind words she loved so well, "Merry Christmas to Jean!" If she could only have lived one day longer!

At last she ran out of money, and would not use mine. So she sent to one of those New York homes for poor girls all the clothes she could spare—and more, most likely.

Christmas Night.—This afternoon they took her away from her room. As soon as I might, I went down to the library, and there she lay, in her coffin, dressed in exactly the same clothes she wore when she stood at the other end of the same room on the 6th of October last, as Clara's chief bridesmaid. Her face was radiant with happy excitement then; it was the same face now, with the dignity of death and the peace of God upon it.

They told me the first mourner to come was the dog. He came uninvited, and stood up on his hind legs and rested his fore paws upon the trestle, and took a last long look at the face that was so dear to him, then went his way as silently as he had come. *He knows.*

At mid-afternoon it began to snow. The pity of it—that Jean could not see it! She so loved the snow.

The snow continued to fall. At six o'clock the hearse drew up to the door to bear away its pathetic burden. As they lifted the casket, Paine began playing on the orchestrelle Shubert's *Impromptu,* which was Jean's favorite. Then he played the

Intermezzo; that was for Susy; then he played the *Largo;* that was for their mother. He did this at my request. Elsewhere in my *Autobiography* I have told how the *Intermezzo* and the *Largo* came to be associated in my heart with Susy and Livy in their last hours in this life.

From my windows I saw the hearse and the carriages wind along the road and gradually grow vague and spectral in the falling snow, and presently disappear. Jean was gone out of my life, and would not come back any more. Jervis, the cousin she had played with when they were babies together—he and her beloved old Katy—were conducting her to her distant childhood home, where she will lie by her mother's side once more, in the company of Susy and Langdon.

December 26th.—The dog came to see me at eight o'clock this morning. He was very affectionate, poor orphan! My room will be his quarters hereafter.

The storm raged all night. It has raged all the morning. The snow drives across the landscape in vast clouds, superb, sublime —and Jean not here to see.

2.30 P.M.—It is the time appointed. The funeral has begun. Four hundred miles away, but I can see it all, just as if I were there. The scene is the library in the Langdon homestead. Jean's coffin stands where her mother and I stood, forty years ago, and were married; and where Susy's coffin stood thirteen years ago; where her mother's stood five years and a half ago; and where mine will stand after a little time.

Five o'clock.—It is all over.

When Clara went away two weeks ago to live in Europe, it was hard, but I could bear it, for I had Jean left. I said *we* would be a family. We said we would be close comrades and happy—just we two. That fair dream was in my mind when Jean met me at the steamer last Monday; it was in my mind when she received me at the door last Tuesday evening. We were together; *we were a family!* the dream had come true—oh, precisely true, contentedly true, satisfyingly true! and remained true two whole days.

And now? Now Jean is in her grave!

In the grave—if I can believe it. God rest her sweet spirit!

HOW I WAS SOLD IN NEWARK

From SKETCHES NEW AND OLD

IT IS seldom pleasant to tell on oneself, but sometimes it is a sort of relief to a man to make a confession. I wish to unburden my mind now, and yet I almost believe that I am moved to do it more because I long to bring censure upon another man than because I desire to pour balm upon my wounded heart. (I don't know what balm is, but I believe it is the correct expression to use in this connection—never having seen any balm.) You may remember that I lectured in Newark lately for the young gentlemen of the —— Society? I did at any rate. During the afternoon of that day I was talking with one of the young gentlemen just referred to, and he said he had an uncle who, from some cause or other, seemed to have grown permanently bereft of all emotion. And with tears in his eyes, this young man said, "Oh, if I could only see him laugh once more! Oh, if I could only see him weep!" I was touched. I could never withstand distress.

I said: "Bring him to my lecture. I'll start him for you."

"Oh, if you could but do it! If you could but do it, all our family would bless you for evermore—for he is so very dear to us. Oh, my benefactor, can you make him laugh? can you bring soothing tears to those parched orbs?"

I was profoundly moved. I said: "My son, bring the old party round. I have got some jokes in that lecture that will make him laugh if there is any laugh in him; and if they miss fire, I have got some others that will make him cry or kill him, one or the other." Then the young man blessed me, and wept on my neck, and went after his uncle. He placed him in full view, in the second row of benches, that night, and I began on him. I tried him with mild jokes, then with severe ones; I dosed him with bad jokes and riddled him with good ones; I fired old stale jokes into him, and peppered him fore and aft with red-hot new ones; I warmed up to my work, and assaulted him on the right and left, in front and behind; I fumed and sweated and charged and ranted till I was hoarse and sick and frantic and furious; but I never moved him once—I never started a smile or a tear! Never a ghost of a smile, and never a suspicion of moisture! I was astounded. I closed the lecture at last with one despairing shriek—with one wild burst of humor, and hurled a joke of supernatural atrocity full at him!

Then I sat down bewildered and exhausted.

The president of the society came up and bathed my head with cold water, and said: "What made you carry on so toward the last?"

I said: "I was trying to make that confounded old fool laugh, in the second row."

And he said: "Well, you were wasting your time, because he is deaf and dumb, and as blind as a badger!"

Now, was that any way for that old man's nephew to impose on a stranger and an orphan like me? I ask you as a man and brother, if that was any way for him to do?

ON THE BABIES

From Mark Twain's Speeches[1]

At the banquet, in Chicago, given by the Army of the Tennessee to their first commander, General U. S. Grant, November, 1879. The fifteenth regular toast was "The Babies—as they comfort us in our sorrows, let us not forget them in our festivities." Mark Twain responded as follows:

I like that. We have not all had the good fortune to be ladies. We have not all been generals, or poets, or statesmen; but when the toast works down to the babies, we stand on common ground. It is a shame that for a thousand years the world's banquets have utterly ignored the baby, as if he didn't amount to anything. If you will stop and think a minute—if you will go back fifty or one hundred years to your early married life and recontemplate your first baby—you will remember that he amounted to a good deal, and even something over. You soldiers all know that when that little fellow arrived at family headquarters you had to hand in your resignation. He took entire command. You became his lackey, his mere body-servant, and you had to stand around, too. He was not a commander who made allowances for time, distance, weather, or anything else. You had to execute his order whether it was possible or not. And there was only one form of marching in his manual of tactics, and that was the double-quick. He treated you with every sort of insolence and disrespect, and the bravest of you didn't dare to say a word. You could face the death-storm at Donelson and Vicksburg, and give back blow for blow; but when he clawed your whiskers, and pulled your hair, and twisted your nose, you had to take it. When the thunders of war were sounding in your ears you set your faces toward the batteries, and advanced with steady tread; but when he turned on the terrors of his war-whoop you advanced in the other direction, and mighty glad of the chance, too. When he called for soothing-syrup, did you venture to throw out any side remarks about certain services being unbecoming an officer and a gentleman? No. You got up and *got* it. When he ordered his pap-bottle and it was not warm, did you talk back? Not you. You went to work and *warmed* it. You even descended so far in your menial office as to take a suck at that warm, insipid stuff yourself, to see if it was right—three parts water to one of milk, a touch of sugar to modify the colic, and a drop of peppermint to kill those hiccoughs. I can taste that stuff yet. And how many things you learned as you went along! Sentimental young folks still take stock in that beautiful old saying that when the baby smiles in his sleep, it is because the angels are whispering to him. Very pretty, but too thin—simply wind on the stomach, my friends. If the baby proposed to take a walk at his usual hour, two o'clock in the morning, didn't you rise up promptly and remark, with a mental addition which would not improve a Sunday-school book *much,* that that was the very thing you were about to propose yourself? Oh! you were under good discipline, and as you went fluttering up and down the room in your undress uniform, you not only prattled undignified baby-talk, but even tuned up your martial voices and tried to *sing!*—"Rock-a-by baby in the treetop," for instance. What a spectacle for an Army of the Tennessee! And what an affliction for the neighbors, too; for it is not everybody within a mile around that likes military music at three in the morning. And when you had been keeping this sort of thing up two or three hours, and your little velvet-head intimated that nothing suited him like exercise and noise, what did you do? [*"Go on!"*] You simply *went* on until you dropped in the last ditch. The idea that a *baby* doesn't *amount* to anything! Why, *one* baby is just a house and a front yard full by itself. *One* baby can furnish more business than you and your whole Interior Department can attend to. He is enterprising, irrepressible, brimful of lawless activities. Do what you please, you can't make him stay on the reservation. Sufficient unto the day is one baby. As long as you are in your right mind don't you ever pray for twins. Twins amount to a permanent riot. And there isn't any real difference between triplets and an insurrection.

Yes, it was high time for a toast-master to recognize the importance of the babies. Think what is in store for the present crop! Fifty years from now we shall all be dead, I trust, and then this flag, if it still survive (and let us hope it may), will be floating over a Republic numbering 200,000,000 souls, according to the settled laws of our increase. Our present schooner of State will have grown into a political leviathan—a *Great*

Eastern.[1] The cradled babies of to-day will be on deck. Let them be well trained, for we are going to leave a big contract on their hands. Among the three or four million cradles now rocking in the land are some which this nation would preserve for ages as sacred things, if we could know which ones they are. In one of these cradles the unconscious Farragut of the future is at this moment teething—think of it!—and putting in a world of dead earnest, unarticulated, but perfectly justifiable profanity over it, too. In another the future renowned astronomer is blinking at the shining Milky Way with but a languid interest—poor little chap!—and wondering what has become of that other one they call the wet-nurse. In another the future great historian is lying—and doubtless will continue to lie until his earthly mission is ended. In another the future President is busying himself with no profounder problem of state than what the mischief has become of his hair so early; and in a mighty array of other cradles there are now some 60,000 future office-seekers, getting ready to furnish him occasion to grapple with that same old problem a second time. And in still one more cradle, somewhere under the flag, the future illustrious commander-in-chief of the American armies is so little burdened with his approaching grandeurs and responsibilities as to be giving his whole strategic mind at this moment to trying to find out some way to get his big toe into his mouth—an achievement which, meaning no disrespect, the illustrious guest of this evening turned *his* entire attention to some fifty-six years ago; and if the child is but a prophecy of the man, there are mighty few who will doubt that he *succeeded.*

[1]A famous steamship of Mark Twain's time. What name might be subsituated to-day?

ABOUT BARBERS

ALL things change except barbers, the ways of barbers, and the surroundings of barbers. These never change. What one experiences in a barber's shop the first time he enters one is what he always experiences in barbers' shops afterward till the end of his days. I got shaved this morning as usual. A man approached the door from Jones Street as I approached it from Main—a thing that always happens. I hurried up, but it was of no use; he entered the door one little step ahead of me, and I followed in on his heels and saw him take the only vacant chair, the one presided over by the best barber. It always happens so. I sat down, hoping that I might fall heir to the chair belonging to the better of the remaining two barbers, for he had already begun combing his man's hair, while his comrade was not yet quite done rubbing up and oiling his customer's locks. I watched the probabilities with strong interest. When I saw that No. 2 was gaining on No. 1 my interest grew to solicitude. When No. 1 stopped a moment to make change on a bath ticket for a new-comer, and lost ground in the race, my solicitude rose to anxiety. When No. 1 caught up again, and both he and his comrade were pulling the towels away and brushing the powder from their customers' cheeks, and it was about an even thing which one would say "Next!" first, my very breath stood still with the suspense. But when at the culminating moment No. 1 stopped to pass a comb a couple of times through his customer's eyebrows, I saw that he had lost the race by a single instant, and I rose indignant and quitted the shop, to keep from falling into the hands of No. 2; for I have none of that enviable firmness that enables a man to look calmly into the eyes of a waiting barber and tell him he will wait for his fellow-barber's chair.

I stayed out fifteen minutes, and then went back, hoping for better luck. Of course all the chairs were occupied now, and four men sat waiting, silent, unsociable, distraught, and looking bored, as men always do who are waiting their turn in a barber's shop. I sat down in one of the iron-armed compartments of an old sofa, and put in the time for a while reading the framed advertisements of all sorts of quack nostrums for dyeing and coloring the hair. Then I read the greasy names on the private bay-rum bottles; read the names and noted the numbers on the private shaving-cups in the pigeonholes; studied the stained and damaged cheap prints on the walls, of battles, early Presidents, and voluptuous recumbent sultanas, and the tiresome and everlasting young girl putting her grandfather's spectacles on; execrated in my heart the cheerful canary and the distracting parrot that few barbers' shops are without. Finally, I searched out the least dilapidated of last year's illustrated papers that littered the foul center-table, and conned their unjustifiable misrepresentations of old forgotten events.

At last my turn came. A voice said "Next!" and I surrendered to—No. 2, of course. It always happens so. I said meekly that I was in a hurry, and it affected him as strongly as if he had never heard it. He shoved up my head, and put a napkin under it. He plowed his fingers into my collar and fixed a towel there. He explored my hair with his claws and suggested that it needed trimming. I said I did not want it trimmed. He explored again and said it was pretty long for the present style—better have a little taken off; it needed it behind especially. I said I had had it cut only a week before. He yearned over it reflectively a moment, and then asked with a disparaging manner, who cut it? I came back at him promptly with a "You did!" I had him there. Then he fell to stirring up his lather and regarding himself in the glass, stopping now and then to get close and examine his chin critically or inspect a pimple. Then he lathered one side of my face thoroughly, and was about to lather the other, when a dog-fight attracted his attention, and he ran to the window and stayed and saw it out, losing two shillings on the result in bets with the other barbers, a thing which gave me great satisfaction. He finished lathering, and then began to rub in the suds with his hand.

He now began to sharpen his razor on an old suspender, and was delayed a good deal on account of a controversy about a cheap masquerade ball he had figured at the night before, in red cambric and bogus ermine, as some kind of a king. He was so gratified with being chaffed about some damsel whom he had smitten with his charms that he used every means to continue the controversy by pretending to be annoyed at the chaffings of his fellows. This matter begot more surveyings of himself in the glass, and he put down his razor and brushed his hair with elaborate care, plastering an inverted arch of it down on his forehead, accomplishing an accurate "part" behind, and brushing the two wings forward over his ears with nice exactness. In the mean time the leather was drying on my face, and apparently eating into my vitals.

Now he began to shave, digging his fingers into my countenance to stretch the skin and bundling and tumbling my head this way and that as convenience in shaving demanded. As long as he was on the tough sides of my face I did not suffer; but when he began to rake, and rip, and tug at my chin, the tears came. He now made a handle of my nose, to assist him shaving the corners of my upper lip, and it was by this bit of circumstantial evidence that I discovered that a part of his duties in the shop was to clean the kerosene-lamps. I had often wondered in an indolent way whether the barbers did that, or whether it was the boss.

About this time I was amusing myself trying to guess where he would be most likely to cut me this time, but he got ahead of me, and sliced me on the end of the chin before I had got my mind made up. He immediately sharpened his razor—he might have done it before. I do not like a close shave, and would not let him go over me a second time. I tried to get him to put up his razor, dreading that he would make for the side of my chin, my pet tender spot, a place which a razor cannot touch twice without making trouble; but he said he only wanted to just smooth off one little roughness, and in the same moment he slipped his razor along the forbidden ground, and the dreaded pimple-signs of a close shave rose up smarting and answered to the call. Now he soaked his towel in bay rum, and slapped it all over my face nastily; slapped it over as if a human being ever yet washed his face in that way. Then he dried it by slapping with the dry part of the towel, as if a human being ever dried his face in such a fashion; but a barber seldom rubs you like a Christian. Next he poked bay rum into the cut place with his towel, then choked the wound with powdered starch, then soaked it with bay rum again, and would have gone on soaking and powdering it forevermore, no doubt, if I had not rebelled and begged off. He powdered my whole face now, straightened me up, and began to plow my hair thoughtfully with his hands. Then he suggested a shampoo, and said my hair needed it badly, very badly. I observed that I shampooed it myself very thoroughly in the bath yesterday. I "had him" again. He next recommended some of "Smith's Hair Glorifier," and offered to sell me a bottle. I declined. He praised the new perfume, "Jones's Delight of the Toilet," and proposed to sell me some of that. I declined again. He tendered me a tooth-wash atrocity of his own invention, and when I declined offered to trade knives with me.

He returned to business after the miscarriage of this last enterprise, sprinkled me all over, legs and all, greased my hair in defiance of my protest against it, rubbed and scrubbed a good deal of it out by the roots, and combed and brushed the rest, parting it behind, and plastering the eternal inverted arch of hair down on my forehead, and then, while combing my scant eyebrows and defiling them with pomade, strung out an account of the achievements of a six-ounce black-and-tan terrier of his till I heard the whistles blow for noon, and knew I was five minutes too late for the train. Then he snatched away the towel, brushed it lightly about my face, passed his comb through my eyebrows once more, and gaily sang out "Next!"

This barber fell down and died of apoplexy two hours later. I am waiting over a day for my revenge—I am going to attend his funeral.

ON THE WEATHER

From MARK TWAIN'S SPEECHES

At the New England Society's seventy-first annual dinner, New York City.

The next toast was: "The Oldest Inhabitant—The Weather of New England."

Who can lose it and forget it?
Who can have it and regret it?
Be interposer 'twixt us Twain.

Merchant of Venice.

To this Mark Twain replied as follows:

I REVERENTLY believe that the Maker who made us all makes everything in New England but the weather. I don't know who makes that, but I think it must be raw apprentices in the weather-clerk's factory who experiment and learn how, in New England, for board and clothes, and then are promoted to make weather for countries that require a good article, and will take their custom elsewhere if they don't get it. There is a sumptuous variety about the New England weather that compels the stranger's admiration—and regret. The weather is always doing something there; always attending strictly to business; always getting up new designs and trying them on the people to see how they will go. But it gets through more business in spring than in any other season. In the spring I have counted one hundred and thirty-six different kinds of weather inside of four-and-twenty hours. It was I that made the fame and fortune of that man that had that marvelous collection of weather on exhibition at the Centennial, that so astounded the foreigners. He was going to travel all over the world and get specimens from all the climes. I said, "Don't you do it; you come to New England on a favorable spring day." I told him what we could do in the way of style, variety, and quantity. Well, he came and he made his collection in four days. As to variety, why, he confessed that he got hundreds of kinds of weather that he had never heard of before. And as to quantity—well, after he had picked out and discarded all that was blemished in any way, he not only had weather enough, but weather to spare; weather to hire out; weather to sell; to deposit; weather to invest; weather to give to the poor. The people of New England are by nature patient and forbearing, but there are some things which they will not stand. Every year they kill a lot of poets for writing about "Beautiful Spring." These are generally casual visitors, who bring their notions of spring from somewhere else, and cannot, of course, know how the natives feel about spring. And so the first thing they know the opportunity to inquire how they feel has permanently gone by. Old Probabilities has a mighty reputation for accurate prophecy, and thoroughly well deserves it. You take up the paper and observe how crisply and confidently he checks off what to-day's weather is going to be on the Pacific, down South, in the Middle States, in the Wisconsin region. See him sail along in the joy and pride of his power till he gets to New England, and then see his tail drop. *He* doesn't know what the weather is going to be in New England. Well, he mulls over it, and by and by he gets out something about like this: Probable northeast to southwest winds, varying to the southward and westward and eastward, and points between, high and low barometer swapping around from place to place; probable areas of rain, snow, hail, and drought, succeeded or preceded by earthquakes, with thunder and lightning. Then he jots down this postscript from his wandering mind, to cover accidents: "But it is possible that the program may be wholly changed in the mean time." Yes, one of the brightest gems in the New England weather is the dazzling uncertainty of it. There is only one thing certain about it: you are certain there is going to be plenty of it—a perfect grand review; but you never can tell which end of the procession is going to move first. You fix up for the drought; you leave your umbrella in the house and sally out, and two to one you get drowned. You make up your mind that the earthquake is due; you stand from under, and take hold of something to steady yourself, and the first thing you know you get struck by lightning. These are great disappointments; but they can't be helped. The lightning there is peculiar; it is so convincing, that when it strikes a thing it doesn't leave enough of that thing behind for you to tell whether—Well, you'd think it was something valuable, and a Congressman had been there. And the thunder. When the thunder begins to merely tune up and scrape and saw, and key up the instruments for the performance, strangers say, "Why, what awful thunder you have here!" But when the baton is raised and the real concert begins, you'll find that stranger down in the cellar with his head in the ash-barrel. Now as to the *size* of the weather in New England—lengthways, I mean. It is utterly disproportioned to the size of that little country. Half the time, when it is packed as full as it can stick, you will see that New England weather sticking out beyond the edges and projecting around hundreds and hundreds of miles over the neighboring states. She can't hold a tenth part of her weather. You can see cracks all about where she has strained herself trying to do it. I could speak volumes about the inhuman perversity of the New England weather, but I will give but a single specimen. I like to hear rain on a tin roof. So I covered part of my roof with tin, with an eye to that luxury. Well, sir, do you think it ever rains on that tin? No, sir; skips it every time. Mind, in this speech I have been trying merely to do honor to the New England weather—no language could do it justice. But, after all, there are at least one or two things about that weather (or, if you please, effects produced by it) which we residents would not like to part with. If we hadn't our bewitching autumn foliage, we should still have to credit the weather with one feature which compensates for all its bullying vagaries—the ice-storm: when a leafless tree is clothed with ice from the bottom to the top—ice that is as bright and clear as crystal; when every bough and twig is strung with ice-beads, frozen dewdrops, and the whole tree sparkles cold and white, like the Shah of Persia's diamond plume. Then the wind waves the branches and the sun comes out and turns all those myriads of beads and drops to prisms that glow and burn and flash with all manner of colored fires, which change and change again with inconceivable rapidity from blue to red, from red to green, and green to gold—the tree becomes a spraying fountain, a very explosion of dazzling jewels; and it stands there the acme, the climax, the supremest possibility in art or nature, of bewildering, intoxicating, intolerable magnificence. One cannot make the words too strong.

CHAPTER VII

COLONEL SELLERS'S SCHEMES FOR MONEY-MAKING

Via, Pecunia! when she's run and gone
And fled, and dead, then will I fetch her again
With aqua vitæ, out of an old hogshead!
While there are lees of wine, or dregs of beer,
I'll never want her! Coin her out of cobwebs,
Dust, but I'll have her! raise wool upon egg-shells,
Sir, and make grass grow out of marrow-bones,
To make her come!

Ben Jonson.

BEARING Washington Hawkins and his fortunes, the stage-coach tore out of Swansea at a fearful gait, with horn tooting gaily and half the town admiring from doors and windows. But it did not tear any more after it got to the outskirts; it dragged along stupidly enough, then—till it came in sight of the next hamlet; and then the bugle tooted gaily again, and again the vehicle went tearing by the houses. This sort of conduct marked every entry to a station and every exit from it; and so in those days children grew up with the idea that stage-coaches always tore and always tooted; but they also grew up with the idea that pirates went into action in their Sunday clothes, carrying the black flag in one hand and pistoling people with the other, merely because they were so represented in the pictures: but these illusions vanished when later years brought their disenchanting wisdom. They learned then that the stage-coach is but a poor, plodding, vulgar thing in the solitudes of the highway; and that the pirate is only a seedy, unfantastic "rough," when he is out of the pictures.

Toward evening, the stage-coach came thundering into Hawkeye with a perfectly triumphant ostentation—which was natural and proper, for Hawkeye was a pretty large town for interior Missouri. Washington, very stiff and tired and hungry, climbed out, and wondered how he was to proceed now. But his difficulty was quickly solved. Colonel Sellers came down the street on a run and arrived panting for breath. He said:

"Lord bless you—I'm glad to see you, Washington—perfectly

delighted to see you, my boy! I got your message. Been on the lookout for you. Heard the stage horn, but had a party I couldn't shake off—man that's got an enormous thing on hand—wants me to put some capital into it—and I tell you, my boy, I could do worse, I could do a deal worse. No, now, let that luggage alone; I'll fix that. Here, Jerry, got anything to do? All right—shoulder this plunder and follow me. Come along, Washington. Lord, I'm glad to see you! Wife and the children are just perishing to look at you. Bless you, they won't know you, you've grown so. Folks all well, I suppose? That's good—glad to hear that. We're always going to run down and see them, but I'm into so many operations, and they're not things a man feels like trusting to other people, and so somehow we keep putting it off. Fortunes in them! Good gracious, it's the country to pile up wealth in! Here we are—here's where the Sellers dynasty hangs out. Dump it on the doorstep, Jerry—the blackest niggro in the state, Washington, but got a good heart—mighty likely boy, is Jerry. And now I suppose you've got to have ten cents, Jerry. That's all right—when a man works for me—when a man—in the other pocket. I reckon—when a man—why, where the mischief *is* that portmonnaie!—when a—well now that's odd—Oh, now I remember, must have left it at the bank; and b' George I've left my check-book, too—Polly says I ought to have a nurse—well, no matter. Let me have a dime, Washington, if you've got—ah, thanks. Now clear out, Jerry, your complexion has brought on the twilight half an hour ahead of time. Pretty fair joke—pretty fair. Here he is, Polly! Washington's come, children!—come now, don't eat him up—finish him in the house. Welcome, my boy, to a mansion that is proud to shelter the son of the best man that walks on the ground. Si Hawkins has been a good friend to me, and I believe I can say that whenever I've had a chance to put him into a good thing I've done it, and done it pretty cheerfully, too. I put him into that sugar speculation—what a grand thing that was, if we hadn't held on too long!"

True enough; but holding on too long had utterly ruined both of them; and the saddest part of it was, that they never had had so much money to lose before, for Sellers's sale of their mule crop that year in New Orleans had been a great financial success. If he had kept out of sugar and gone back home content to stick to mules it would have been a happy wisdom. As it was, he managed to kill two birds with one stone—that is to say, he killed the sugar speculation by holding for high rates till he had to sell at the bottom figure, and that calamity killed the mule that laid the golden egg—which is but a figurative expression and will be so understood. Sellers had returned home cheerful but empty-handed, and the mule business lapsed into other hands. The sale of the Hawkins property by the sheriff had followed, and the Hawkins hearts been torn to see Uncle Dan'l and his wife pass from the auction-block into the hands of a negro trader and depart for the remote South to be seen no more by the family. It had seemed like seeing their own flesh and blood sold into banishment.

Washington was greatly pleased with the Sellers mansion. It was a two-story-and-a-half brick, and much more stylish than any of its neighbors. He was borne to the family sitting-room in triumph by the swarm of little Sellerses, the parents following with their arms about each other's waists.

The whole family were poorly and cheaply dressed; and the clothing, although neat and clean, showed many evidences of having seen long service. The Colonel's "stovepipe" hat was napless and shiny with much polishing, but nevertheless it had an almost convincing expression about it of having been just purchased new. The rest of his clothing was napless and shiny, too, but it had the air of being entirely satisfied with itself and blandly sorry for other people's clothes. It was growing rather dark in the house, and the evening air was chilly, too. Sellers said:

Lay off your overcoat, Washington, and draw up to the stove and make yourself at home—just consider yourself under your own shingles, my boy—I'll have a fire going, in a jiffy. Light the lamp, Polly, dear, and let's have things cheerful—just as glad to see you, Washington, as if you'd been lost a century and we'd found you again!"

By this time the Colonel was conveying a lighted match into a poor little stove. Then he propped the stove-door to its place by leaning the poker against it, for the hinges had retired from business. This door framed a small square of isinglass, which now warmed up with a faint glow. Mrs. Sellers lit a cheap, showy lamp, which dissipated a good deal of the gloom, and then everybody gathered into the light and took the stove into close companionship.

The children climbed all over Sellers, fondled him, petted him, and were lavishly petted in return. Out from this tugging, laughing, chattering disguise of legs and arms and little faces, the Colonel's voice worked its way and his tireless tongue ran blithely on without interruption; and the purring little wife, diligent with her knitting, sat near at hand and looked happy and proud and grateful; and she listened as one who listens to oracles and gospels and whose grateful soul is being refreshed with the bread of life. By and by the children quieted down to listen; clustered about their father, and resting their elbows on his legs, they hung upon his words as if he were uttering the music of the spheres.

A dreary old haircloth sofa against the wall; a few damaged chairs; the small table the lamp stood on; the crippled stove—these things constituted the furniture of the room. There was no carpet on the floor; on the wall were occasional square-shaped interruptions of the general tint of the plaster which betrayed that there used to be pictures in the house—but there were none now. There were no mantel ornaments, unless one might bring himself to regard as an ornament a clock which never came within fifteen strokes of striking the right time, and whose hands always hitched together at twenty-two minutes past anything and traveled in company the rest of the way home.

"Remarkable clock!" said Sellers, and got up and wound it. "I've been offered—well, I wouldn't expect you to believe what I've been offered for that clock. Old Governor Hager never sees me but he says, 'Come, now, Colonel, name your price—I *must* have that clock!' But my goodness I'd as soon think of selling my wife. As I was saying to—silence in the court, now, she's begun to strike! You can't talk against her—you have to just be patient and hold up till she's said her say. Ah—well, as I was saying, when—she's beginning again! Nineteen, twenty, twenty-one, twenty-two, twen—ah, that's all. Yes, as I was saying to old Judge—go it, old girl, don't mind me. Now how is that? Isn't that a good, spirited tone? She can wake the dead! Sleep? Why you might as well try to sleep in a thunder factory. Now just listen at that. She'll strike a hundred and fifty, now, without stopping—you'll see. There ain't another clock like that in Christendom."

Washington hoped that this might be true, for the din was distracting—though the family, one and all, seemed filled with joy; and the more the clock "buckled down to her work" as the Colonel expressed it, and the more insupportable the clatter became, the more enchanted they all appeared to be. When there was silence, Mrs. Sellers lifted upon Washington a face that beamed with a childlike pride, and said:

"It belonged to his grandmother."

The look and the tone were a plain call for admiring surprise, and therefore Washington said—(it was the only thing that offered itself at the moment):

"Indeed!"

"Yes, it did, didn't it, father!" exclaimed one of the twins. "She was my great-grandmother—and George's too; wasn't she, father! *You* never saw her, but Sis has seen her, when Sis was a baby—didn't you, Sis! Sis has seen her most a hundred times. She was awful deef—she's dead, now. Ain't she, father!"

All the children chimed in, now, with one general Babel of information about deceased—nobody offering to read the riot act or seeming to discountenance the insurrection or disapprove of it in any way—but the head twin drowned all the turmoil and held his own against the field:

"It's our clock, now—and it's got wheels inside of it, and a thing that flutters every time she strikes — don't it, father! Great-grandmother died before hardly any of us were born—she was an Old-School Baptist and had warts all over her—you ask father if she didn't. She had an uncle once that was bald-headed and used to have fits; he wasn't *our* uncle, I don't know what he was to us—some kin or another I reckon—father's seen him a thousand times—hain't you, father! We used to have a calf that et apples and just chawed up dishrags like nothing, and if you stay here you'll see lots of funerals—won't he, Sis! Did you ever see a house afire? I have! Once me and Jim Terry—"

But Sellers began to speak now, and the storm ceased. He began to tell about an enormous speculation he was thinking of embarking some capital in—a speculation which some London bankers had been over to consult with him about—and soon he was building glittering pyramids of coin, and Washington was presently growing opulent under the magic of his eloquence. But at the same time Washington was not able to ignore the cold entirely. He was nearly as close to the stove as he could get, and yet he could not pursuade himself that he felt the slightest heat, notwithstanding the isinglass door was still gently and serenely glowing. He tried to get a trifle closer to the stove, and the consequence was, he tripped the supporting poker and the stove-door tumbled to the floor. And then there was a revelation—there was nothing in the stove but a lighted tallow candle!

The poor youth blushed and felt as if he must die with shame. But the Colonel was only disconcerted for a moment—he straightway found his voice again:

"A little idea of my own, Washington—one of the greatest things in the world! You must write and tell your father about it—don't forget that, now. I have been reading up some European scientific reports—friend of mine, Count Fugier, sent them to me—sends me all sorts of things from Paris—he thinks the world of me, Fugier does. Well, I saw that the Academy of France had been testing the properties of heat, and they came to the conclusion that it was a non-conductor or something like that, and of course its influence must necessarily be deadly in nervous organizations with excitable temperaments, especially where there is any tendency toward rheumatic affections. Bless you, I saw in a moment what was the matter with us, and says I, out goes your fires!—no more slow torture and certain death for me, sir. What you want is the *appearance* of heat, not the heat itself—that's the idea. Well, how to do it was the next thing. I just put my head to work, pegged away a couple of days, and here you are! Rheumatism? Why a man can't any more start a case of rheumatism in this house than he can shake an opinion out of a mummy! Stove with a candle in it and a transparent door—that's it—it has been the salvation of this family. Don't you fail to write your father about it, Washington. And tell him the idea is mine—I'm no more conceited than most people, I reckon, but you know it is human nature for a man to want credit for a thing like that."

Washington said with his blue lips that he would, but he said in his secret heart that he would promote no such iniquity. He tried to believe in the healthfulness of the invention, and succeeded tolerably well; but after all he could not feel that good health in a frozen body was any real improvement on the rheumatism.

THE STOLEN WHITE ELEPHANT[1]

From Tom Sawyer Abroad, Tom Sawyer Detective and Other Stories[2]

I

THE following curious history was related to me by a chance railway acquaintance. He was a gentleman more than seventy years of age, and his thoroughly good and gentle face and earnest and sincere manner imprinted the unmistakable stamp of truth upon every statement which fell from his lips. He said:

You know in what reverence the royal white elephant of Siam is held by the people of that country. You know it is sacred to kings, only kings may possess it, and that it is, indeed, in a measure even superior to kings, since it receives not merely honor but worship. Very well; five years ago, when the troubles concerning the frontier line arose between Great Britain and Siam, it was presently manifest that Siam had been in the wrong. Therefore every reparation was quickly made, and the British representative stated that he was satisfied and the past should be forgotten. This greatly relieved the King of Siam, and partly as a token of gratitude, but partly also, perhaps, to wipe out any little remaining vestige of unpleasantness which England might feel toward him, he wished to send the Queen a present—the sole sure way of propitiating an enemy, according to Oriental ideas. This present ought not only to be a royal one, but transcendently royal. Wherefore, what offering could be so meet as that of a white elephant? My position in the Indian civil service was such that I was deemed peculiarly worthy of the honor of conveying the present to her Majesty. A ship was fitted out for me and my servants and the officers and

[1] Left out of *A Tramp Abroad,* because it was feared that some of the particulars had been exaggerated, and that others were not true. Before these suspicions had been proven groundless, the book had gone to press.—M. T.

attendants of the elephant, and in due time I arrived in New York harbor and placed my royal charge in admirable quarters in Jersey City. It was necessary to remain awhile in order to recruit the animal's health before resuming the voyage.

All went well during a fortnight—then my calamities began. The white elephant was stolen! I was called up at dead of night and informed of this fearful misfortune. For some moments I was beside myself with terror and anxiety; I was helpless. Then I grew calmer and collected my faculties. I soon saw my course—for, indeed, there was but the one course for an intelligent man to pursue. Late as it was, I flew to New York and got a policeman to conduct me to the headquarters of the detective force. Fortunately I arrived in time, though the chief of the force, the celebrated Inspector Blunt, was just on the point of leaving for his home. He was a man of middle size and compact frame, and when he was thinking deeply he had a way of knitting his brows and tapping his forehead reflectively with his finger, which impressed you at once with the conviction that you stood in the presence of a person of no common order. The very sight of him gave me confidence and made me hopeful. I stated my errand. It did not flurry him in the least; it had no more visible effect upon his iron self-possession than if I had told him somebody had stolen my dog. He motioned me to a seat, and said, calmly:

"Allow me to think a moment, please."

So saying, he sat down at his office table and leaned his head upon his hand. Several clerks were at work at the other end of the room; the scratching of their pens was all the sound I heard during the next six or seven minutes. Meantime the inspector sat there, buried in thought. Finally he raised his head, and there was that in the firm lines of his face which showed me that his brain had done its work and his plan was made. Said he—and his voice was low and impressive:

"This is no ordinary case. Every step must be warily taken, each step must be made sure before the next is ventured. And secrecy must be observed—secrecy profound and absolute. Speak to no one about the matter, not even the reporters. I will take care of *them;* I will see that they get only what it may suit my ends to let them know." He touched a bell; a youth appeared. "Alaric, tell the reporters to remain for the present." The boy retired. "Now let us proceed to business—and systematically. Nothing can be accomplished in this trade of mine without strict and minute method."

He took a pen and some paper. "Now—name of the elephant?"

"Hassan Ben Ali Ben Selim Abdallah Mohammed Moisé Alhammal Jamsetjejeebhoy Dhuleep Sultan Ebu Bhudpoor."

"Very well. Given name?"

"Jumbo."

"Very well. Place of birth?"

"The capital city of Siam."

"Parents living?"

"No—dead."

"Had they any other issue besides this one?"

"None. He was an only child."

"Very well. These matters are sufficient under that head. Now please describe the elephant, and leave out no particular, however insignificant—that is, insignificant from *your* point of view. To men in my profession there *are* no insignificant particulars; they do not exist."

I described—he wrote. When I was done, he said:

"Now listen. If I have made any mistakes, correct me."

He read as follows:

"Height, 19 feet; length from apex of forehead to insertion of tail, 26 feet; length of trunk, 16 feet; length of tail, 6 feet; total length, including trunk and tail, 48 feet; length of tusks, 9½ feet; ears in keeping with these dimensions; footprint resembles the mark left when one up-ends a barrel in the snow; color of the elephant, a dull white; has a hole the size of a plate in each ear for the insertion of jewelry, and possesses the habit in a remarkable degree of squirting water upon spectators and of maltreating with his trunk not only such persons as he is acquainted with, but even entire strangers; limps slightly with his right hind leg, and has a small scar in his left armpit caused by a former boil; had on, when stolen, a castle containing seats for fifteen persons, and a gold-cloth saddle-blanket the size of an ordinary carpet."

There were no mistakes. The inspector touched the bell, handed the description to Alaric, and said:

"Have fifty thousand copies of this printed at once and mailed to every detective office and pawnbroker's shop on the continent." Alaric retired. "There—so far, so good. Next, I must have a photograph of the property."

I gave him one. He examined it critically, and said:

"It must do, since we can do no better; but he has his trunk curled up and tucked into his mouth. That is unfortunate, and is calculated to mislead, for of course he does not usually have it in that position." He touched his bell.

"Alaric, have fifty thousand copies of this photograph made the first thing in the morning, and mail them with the descriptive circulars."

Alaric retired to execute his orders. The inspector said:

"It will be necessary to offer a reward, of course. Now as to the amount?"

"What sum would you suggest?"

"To *begin* with, I should say—well, twenty-five thousand dollars. It is an intricate and difficult business; there are a thousand avenues of escape and opportunities of concealment. These thieves have friends and pals everywhere——"

"Bless me, do you know who they are?"

The wary face, practised in concealing the thoughts and feelings within, gave me no token, nor yet the replying words, so quietly uttered:

"Never mind about that. I may, and I may not. We generally gather a pretty shrewd inkling of who our man is by the manner of his work and the size of the game he goes after. We are not dealing with a pickpocket or a hall thief now, make up your mind to that. This property was not 'lifted' by a novice. But, as I was saying, considering the amount of travel which will have to be done, and the diligence with which the thieves will cover up their traces as they move along, twenty-five thousand may be too small a sum to offer, yet I think it worth while to start with that."

So we determined upon that figure as a beginning. Then this man, whom nothing escaped which could by any possibility be made to serve as a clue, said:

"There are cases in detective history to show that criminals have been detected through peculiarities in their appetites. Now, what does this elephant eat, and how much?"

"Well, as to *what* he eats—he will eat *anything*. He will eat a man, he will eat a Bible—he will eat anything *between* a man and a Bible."

"Good—very good, indeed, but too general. Details are necessary—details are the only valuable things in our trade. Very well—as to men. At one meal—or, if you prefer, during one day—how many men will he eat, if fresh?"

"He would not care whether they were fresh or not; at a single meal he would eat five ordinary men."

"Very good; five men; we will put that down. What nationalities would he prefer?"

"He is indifferent about nationalities. He prefers acquaintances, but is not prejudiced against strangers."

"Very good. Now, as to Bibles. How many Bibles would he eat at a meal?"

"He would eat an entire edition."

"It is hardly succinct enough. Do you mean the ordinary octavo, or the family illustrated?"

"I think he would be indifferent to illustrations; that is, I think he would not value illustrations above simple letter-press."

"No, you do not get my idea. I refer to bulk. The ordinary octavo Bible weights about two pounds and a half, while the great quarto with the illustrations weighs ten or twelve. How many Doré Bibles would he eat at a meal?"

"If you knew this elephant, you could not ask. He would take what they had."

"Well, put it in dollars and cents, then. We must get at it somehow. The Doré costs a hundred dollars a copy, Russia leather, beveled."

"He would require about fifty thousand dollars' worth—say an edition of five hundred copies."

"Now that is more exact. I will put that down. Very well; he likes men and Bibles; so far, so good. What else will he eat? I want particulars."

"He will leave Bibles to eat bricks, he will leave bricks to eat bottles, he will leave bottles to eat clothing, he will leave clothing to eat cats, he will leave cats to eat oysters, he will leave oysters to eat ham, he will leave ham to eat sugar, he will leave sugar to eat pie, he will leave pie to eat potatoes, he will leave potatoes to eat bran, he will leave bran to eat hay, he will leave hay to eat oats, he will leave oats to eat rice, for he was mainly raised on it. There is nothing whatever that he will not eat but European butter, and he would eat that if he could taste it."

"Very good. General quantity at a meal—say about——"

"Well, anywhere from a quarter to half a ton."

"And he drinks——"

"Everything that is fluid. Milk, water, whisky, molasses, castor oil, camphene, carbolic acid—it is no use to go into particulars; whatever fluid occurs to you set it down. He will drink anything that is fluid, except European coffee."

"Very good. As to quantity?"

"Put it down five to fifteen barrels—his thirst varies; his other appetites do not."

"These things are unusual. They ought to furnish quite good clues toward tracing him."

He touched the bell.

"Alaric, summon Captain Burns."

Burns appeared. Inspector Blunt unfolded the whole matter to him, detail by detail. Then he said in the clear, decisive tones of a man whose plans are clearly defined in his head and who is accustomed to command:

"Captain Burns, detail Detectives Jones, Davis, Halsey, Bates, and Hackett to shadow the elephant."

"Yes, sir."

"Detail Detectives Moses, Dakin, Murphy, Rogers, Tupper, Higgins, and Bartholomew to shadow the thieves."

"Yes, sir."

"Place a strong guard—a guard of thirty picked men, with a relief of thirty—over the place from whence the elephant was stolen, to keep strict watch there night and day, and allow none to approach—except reporters—without written authority from me."

"Yes, sir."

"Place detectives in plain clothes in the railway, steamship, and ferry depots, and upon all roadways leading out of Jersey City, with orders to search all suspicious persons."

"Yes, sir."

"Furnish all these men with photograph and accompanying description of the elephant, and instruct them to search all trains and outgoing ferryboats and other vessels."

"Yes, sir."

"If the elephant should be found, let him be seized, and the information forwarded to me by telegraph."

"Yes, sir."

"Let me be informed at once if any clues should be found—footprints of the animal, or anything of that kind."

"Yes, sir."

"Get an order commanding the harbor police to patrol the frontages vigilantly."

"Yes, sir."

"Despatch detectives in plain clothes over all the railways, north as far as Canada, west as far as Ohio, south as far as Washington."

"Yes, sir."

"Place experts in all the telegraph offices to listen to all messages; and let them require that all cipher despatches be interpreted to them."

"Yes, sir."

"Let all these things be done with the utmost secrecy—mind, the most impenetrable secrecy."

"Yes, sir."

"Report to me promptly at the usual hour."

"Yes, sir."

"Go!"

"Yes, sir."

He was gone.

Inspector Blunt was silent and thoughtful a moment, while the fire in his eye cooled down and faded out. Then he turned to me and said in a placid voice:

"I am not given to boasting, it is not my habit; but—we shall find the elephant."

I shook him warmly by the hand and thanked him; and I *felt* my thanks, too. The more I had seen of the man the more I liked him and the more I admired him and marveled over the mysterious wonders of his profession. Then we parted for the night, and I went home with a far happier heart than I had carried with me to his office.

II

Next morning it was all in the newspapers, in the minutest detail. It even had additions—consisting of Detective This, Detective That, and Detective The Other's "Theory" as to how the robbery was done, who the robbers were, and whither they had flown with their booty. There were eleven of these theories, and they covered all the possibilities; and this single fact shows what independent thinkers detectives are. No two theories were alike, or even much resembled each other, save in one striking particular, and in that one all the eleven theories were absolutely agreed. That was, that although the rear of my building was torn out and the only door remained locked, the elephant had not been removed through the rent, but by some other (undiscovered) outlet. All agreed that the robbers had made that rent only to mislead the detectives. That never would have occurred to me or to any other layman, perhaps, but it had not deceived the detectives for a moment. Thus, what I had supposed was the only thing that had no mystery about it was in fact the very thing I had gone furthest astray in. The eleven theories all named the supposed robbers, but no two named the same robbers; the total number of suspected persons was thirty-seven. The various newspaper accounts all closed with the most important opinion of all—that of Chief Inspector Blunt. A portion of this statement read as follows:

> The chief knows who the two principals are, namely, "Brick" Duffy and "Red" McFadden. Ten days before the robbery was achieved he was already aware that it was to be attempted, and had quietly proceeded to shadow these two noted villains; but unfortunately on the night in question their track was lost, and before it could be found again the bird was flown—that is, the elephant.
>
> Duffy and McFadden are the boldest scoundrels in the profession; the chief has reasons for believing that they are the men who stole the stove out of the detective headquarters on a bitter night last winter—in consequence of which the chief and every detective present were in the hands of the physicians before morning, some with frozen feet, others with frozen fingers, ears, and other members.

When I read the first half of that I was more astonished than ever at the wonderful sagacity of this strange man. He not only saw everything in the present with a clear eye, but even the future could not be hidden from him. I was soon at his office, and said I could not help wishing he had had those men arrested, and so prevented the trouble and loss; but his reply was simple and unanswerable:

"It is not our province to prevent crime, but to punish it. We cannot punish it until it is committed."

I remarked that the secrecy with which we had begun had been marred by the newspapers; not only all our facts but all our plans and purposes had been revealed; even all the suspected persons had been named; these would doubtless disguise themselves now, or go into hiding.

"Let them. They will find that when I am ready for them my hand will descend upon them, in their secret places, as unerringly as the hand of fate. As to the newspapers, we *must* keep in with them. Fame, reputation, constant public mention—these are the detective's bread and butter. He must publish his facts, else he will be supposed to have none; he must publish his theory, for nothing is so strange or striking as a detective's theory, or brings him so much wonderful respect; we must publish our plans, for these the journals insist upon having, and we could not deny them without offending. We must constantly show the public what we are doing, or they will believe we are doing nothing. It is much pleasanter to have a newspaper say, 'Inspector Blunt's ingenious and extraordinary theory is as follows,' than to have it say some harsh thing, or, worse still, some sarcastic one."

"I see the force of what you say. But I noticed that in one part of your remarks in the papers this morning you refused to reveal your opinion upon a certain minor point."

"Yes, we always do that; it has a good effect. Besides, I had not formed any opinion on that point, anyway."

I deposited a considerable sum of money with the inspector, to meet current expenses, and sat down to wait for news. We were expecting the telegrams to begin to arrive at any moment now. Meantime I reread the newspapers and also our descriptive circular, and observed that our twenty-five thousand dollars reward seemed to be offered only to detectives. I said I thought it ought to be offered to anybody who would catch the elephant. The inspector said:

"It is the detectives who will find the elephant, hence the reward will go to the right place. If other people found the animal, it would only be by watching the detectives and taking advantage of clues and indications stolen from them, and that would entitle the detectives to the reward, after all. The proper office of a reward is to stimulate the men who deliver up their time and their trained sagacities to this sort of work, and not to confer benefits upon chance citizens who stumble upon a capture without having earned the benefits by their own merits and labors."

This was reasonable enough, certainly. Now the telegraphic machine in the corner began to click, and the following despatch was the result:

FLOWER STATION, N. Y., 7.30 A.M.

> Have got a clue. Found a succession of deep tracks across a farm near here. Followed them two miles east without result; think elephant went west. Shall now shadow him in that direction. DARLEY, *Detective.*

"Darley's one of the best men on the force," said the inspector. "We shall hear from him again before long."

Telegram No. 2 came:

BARKER'S, N. J., 7.40 A.M.

Just arrived. Glass factory broken open here during night, and eight hundred bottles taken. Only water in large quantity near here is five miles distant. Shall strike for there. Elephant will be thirsty. Bottles were empty.

BAKER, *Detective.*

"That promises well, too," said the inspector. "I told you the creature's appetites would not be bad clues."

Telegram No. 3:

TAYLORVILLE, L. I., 8.15 A.M.

A haystack near here disappeared during night. Probably eaten. Have got a clue, and am off.

HUBBARD, *Detective.*

"How he does move around!" said the inspector. "I knew we had a difficult job on hand, but we shall catch him yet."

FLOWER STATION, N. Y., 9 A.M.

Shadowed the tracks three miles westward. Large, deep, and ragged. Have just met a farmer who says they are not elephant tracks. Says they are holes where he dug up saplings for shade-trees when ground was frozen last winter. Give me orders how to proceed.

DARLEY, *Detective.*

"Aha! a confederate of the thieves! The thing grows warm," said the inspector.

He dictated the following telegram to Darley:

Arrest the man and force him to name his pals. Continue to follow the tracks—to the Pacific, if necessary.

Chief BLUNT.

Next telegram:

CONEY POINT, PA., 8.45 A.M.

Gas office broken open here during night and three months' unpaid gas bills taken. Have got a clue and am away.

MURPHY, *Detective.*

"Heavens!" said the inspector; "would he eat gas bills?"

"Through ignorance—yes; but they cannot support life. At least, unassisted."

Now came this exciting telegram

IRONVILLE, N. Y., 9.30 A.M.

Just arrived. This village in consternation. Elephant passed through here at five this morning. Some say he went east, some say west, some north, some south—but all say they did not wait to notice particularly. He killed a horse; have secured a piece of it for a clue. Killed it with his trunk; from style of blow, think he struck it left-handed. From position in which horse lies, think elephant traveled northward along line of Berkley Railway. Has four and a half hours' start, but I move on his track at once.

HAWES, *Detective.*

I uttered exclamations of joy. The inspector was as self-contained as a graven image. He calmly touched his bell.

"Alaric, send Captain Burns here."

Burns appeared.

"How many men are ready for instant orders?"

"Ninety-six, sir."

"Send them north at once. Let them concentrate along the line of the Berkley road north of Ironville."

"Yes, sir."

"Let them conduct their movements with the utmost secrecy. As fast as others are at liberty, hold them for orders."

"Yes, sir."

"Go!"

"Yes, sir."

Presently came another telegram:

SAGE CORNERS, N. Y., 10.30.

Just arrived. Elephant passed through here at 8.15. All escaped from the town but a policeman. Apparently elephant did not strike at policeman, but at the lamp-post. Got both. I have secured a portion of the policeman as clue.

STUMM, *Detective.*

"So the elephant has turned westward," said the inspector. "However, he will not escape, for my men are scattered all over that region."

The next telegram said:

GLOVER'S, 11.15.

Just arrived. Village deserted, except sick and aged. Elephant passed through three-quarters of an hour ago.

The anti-temperance mass-meeting was in session; he put his trunk in at a window and washed it out with water from cistern. Some swallowed it—since dead; several drowned. Detectives Cross and O'Shaughnessy were passing through town, but going south—so missed elephant. Whole region for many miles around in terror—people flying from their homes. Wherever they turn they meet elephant, and many are killed. BRANT, *Detective.*

I could have shed tears, this havoc so distressed me. But the inspector only said:

"You see—we are closing in on him. He feels our presence; he has turned eastward again."

Yet further troublous news was in store for us. The telegraph brought this:

HOGANSPORT, 12.19.

Just arrived. Elephant passed through half an hour ago, creating wildest fright and excitement. Elephant raged around streets; two plumbers going by, killed one—other escaped. Regret general. O'FLAHERTY, *Detective.*

"Now he is right in the midst of my men," said the inspector. "Nothing can save him."

A succession of telegrams came from detectives who were scattered through New Jersey and Pennsylvania and who were following clues consisting of ravaged barns, factories, and Sunday-school libraries, with high hopes—hopes amounting to certainties, indeed. The inspector said:

"I wish I could communicate with them and order them north, but that is impossible. A detective only visits a telegraph office to send his report; then he is off again, and you don't know where to put your hand on him."

Now came this despatch:

BRIDGEPORT, CT., 12.15.

Barnum offers rate of $4,000 a year for exclusive privilege of using elephant as traveling advertising medium from now till detectives find him. Wants to paste circus-posters on him. Desires immediate answer.

BOGGS, *Detective.*

"That is perfectly absurd!" I exclaimed.

"Of course it is," said the inspector. "Evidently Mr. Barnum, who thinks he is so sharp, does not know me—but I know him."

Then he dictated this answer to the despatch:

Mr. Barnum's offer declined. Make it $7,000 or nothing.
Chief BLUNT.

"There. We shall not have to wait long for an answer. Mr. Barnum is not at home; he is in the telegraph office—it is his way when he has business on hand. Inside of three ——"

Done.—P. T. BARNUM.

So interrupted the clicking telegraphic instrument. Before I could make a comment upon this extraordinary episode, the following despatch carried my thoughts into another and very distressing channel:

BOLIVIA, N. Y., 12.50.

Elephant arrived here from the south and passed through toward the forest at 11.50, dispersing a funeral on the way, and diminishing the mourners by two. Citizens fired some small cannon-balls into him, and then fled. Detective Burke and I arrived ten minutes later, from the north, but mistook some excavations for footprints, and so lost a good deal of time; but at last we struck the right trail and followed it to the woods. We then got down on our hands and knees and continued to keep a sharp eye on the track, and so shadowed it into the brush. Burke was in advance. Unfortunately the animal had stopped to rest; therefore, Burke having his head down, intent upon the track, butted up against the elephant's hind legs before he was aware of his vicinity. Burke instantly arose to his feet, seized the tail, and exclaimed joyfully, "I claim the re—" but got no further, for a single blow of the huge trunk laid the brave fellow's fragments low in death. I fled rearward, and the elephant, turned and shadowed me to the edge of the wood, making tremendous speed, and I should inevitably have been lost, but that the remains of the funeral providentially intervened again and diverted his attention. I have just learned that nothing of that funeral is now left; but this is no loss, for there is abundance of material for another. Meantime, the elephant has disappeared again.

MULROONEY, *Detective.*

We heard no news except from the diligent and confident detectives scattered about New Jersey, Pennsylvania, Delaware, and Virginia—who were all following fresh and encouraging clues—until shortly after 2 P.M., when this telegram came:

BAXTER CENTER, 2.15.

Elephant been here, plastered over with circus-bills, and broke up a revival, striking down and damaging many who were on the point of entering upon a better life. Citizens penned him up and established a guard. When Detective Brown and I arrived, some time after, we entered inclosure and proceeded to identify elephant by photograph and description. All marks tallied exactly except one, which we could not see—the boil-scar under armpit. To make sure, Brown crept under to look, and was immediately brained—that is, head crushed and destroyed, though nothing issued from debris. All fled; so did elephant, striking right and left with much effect. Has escaped, but left bold blood-track from cannon-wounds. Rediscovery certain. He broke southward, through a dense forest.

BRENT, *Detective.*

That was the last telegram. At nightfall a fog shut down which was so dense that objects but three feet away could not be discerned. This lasted all night. The ferryboats and even the omnibuses had to stop running.

III

Next morning the papers were as full of detective theories as before; they had all our tragic facts in detail also, and a great many more which they had received from their telegraphic correspondents. Column after column was occupied, a third of its way down, with glaring head-lines, which it made my heart sick to read. Their general tone was like this:

THE WHITE ELEPHANT AT LARGE! HE MOVES UPON HIS FATAL MARCH! WHOLE VILLAGES DESERTED BY THEIR FRIGHT-STRICKEN OCCUPANTS! PALE TERROR GOES BEFORE HIM, DEATH AND DEVASTATION FOLLOW AFTER! AFTER THESE, THE DETECTIVES! BARNS DESTROYED, FACTORIES GUTTED, HARVESTS DEVOURED, PUBLIC ASSEMBLAGES DISPERSED, ACCOMPANIED BY SCENES OF CARNAGE IMPOSSIBLE TO DESCRIBE! THEORIES OF THIRTY-FOUR OF THE MOST DISTINGUISHED DETECTIVES ON THE FORCE! THEORY OF CHIEF BLUNT!

"There!" said Inspector Blunt, almost betrayed into excitement, "this is magnificent! This is the greatest windfall that any detective organization ever had. The fame of it will travel to the ends of the earth, and endure to the end of time, and my name with it."

But there was no joy for me. I felt as if I had committed all those red crimes, and that the elephant was only my irresponsible agent. And how the list had grown! In one place he had "interfered with an election and killed five repeaters." He had followed this act with the destruction of two poor fellows, named O'Donohue and McFlannigan, who had "found a refuge in the home of the oppressed of all lands only the day before, and were in the act of exercising for the first time the noble right of American citizens at the polls, when stricken down by the relentless hand of the Scourge of Siam." In another, he had "found a crazy sensation-preacher preparing his next season's heroic attacks on the dance, the theater, and other things which can't strike back, and had stepped on him." And in still another place he had "killed a lightning-rod agent." And so the list went on, growing redder and redder, and more and more heartbreaking. Sixty persons had been killed, and two hundred and forty wounded. All the accounts bore just testimony to the activity and devotion of the detectives, and all closed with the remark that "three hundred thousand citizens and four detectives saw the dread creature, and two of the latter he destroyed."

I dreaded to hear the telegraphic instrument begin to click again. By and by the messages began to pour in, but I was happily disappointed in their nature. It was soon apparent that all trace of the elephant was lost. The fog had enabled him to search out a good hidingplace unobserved. Telegrams from the most absurdly distant points reported that a dim vast mass had been glimpsed there through the fog at such and such an hour, and was "undoubtedly the elephant." This dim vast mass had been glimpsed in New Haven, in New Jersey, in Pennsylvania, in interior New York, in Brooklyn, and even in the city of New York itself! But in all cases the dim vast mass had vanished quickly and left no trace. Every detective of the large force scattered over this huge extent of country sent his hourly report, and each and every one of them had a clue, and was shadowing something, and was hot upon the heels of it.

But the day passed without other result.

The next day the same.

The next just the same.

The newspaper reports began to grow monotonous with facts that amounted to nothing, clues which led to nothing, and theories which had nearly exhausted the elements which surprise and delight and dazzle.

By advice of the inspector I doubled the reward.

Four more dull days followed. Then came a bitter blow to the poor, hard-working detectives—the journalists declined to print their theories, and coldly said, "Give us a rest."

Two weeks after the elephant's disappearance I raised the reward to seventy-five thousand dollars by the inspector's advice. It was a great sum, but I felt that I would rather sacrifice my whole private fortune than lose my credit with my government. Now that the detectives were in adversity, the newspapers turned upon them, and began to fling the most stinging sarcasms at them. This gave the minstrels an idea, and they dressed themselves as detectives and hunted the elephant on the stage in the most extravagant way. The caricaturists made pictures of detectives scanning the country with spyglasses, while the elephant, at their backs, stole apples out of their pockets. And they made all sorts of ridiculous pictures of the detective badge—you have seen that badge printed in gold on the back of detective novels, no doubt—it is a wide-staring eye, with the legend, "WE NEVER SLEEP." When detectives called for a drink, the would-be facetious barkeeper resurrected an obsolete form of expression and said, "Will you have an eye-opener?" All the air was thick with sarcasms.

But there was one man who moved calm, untouched, unaffected, through it all. It was that heart of oak, the chief inspector. His brave eye never drooped, his serene confidence never wavered. He always said:

"Let them rail on; he laughs best who laughs last."

My admiration for the man grew into a species of worship. I was at his side always. His office had become an unpleasant place to me, and now became daily more and more so. Yet if he could endure it I meant to do so also—at least, as long as I could. So I came regularly, and stayed—the only outsider who seemed to be capable of it. Everybody wondered how I could; and often it seemed to me that I must desert, but at such times I looked into that calm and apparently unconscious face, and held my ground.

About three weeks after the elephant's disappearance I was about to say, one morning, that I should *have* to strike my colors and retire, when the great detective arrested the thought by proposing one more superb and masterly move.

This was to compromise with the robbers. The fertility of this man's invention exceeded anything I have ever seen, and I have had a wide intercourse with the world's finest minds. He said he was confident he could compromise for one hundred thousand dollars and recover the elephant. I said I believed I could scrape the amount together, but what would become of the poor detectives who had worked so faithfully? He said:

"In compromises they always get half."

Ths removed my only objection. So the inspector wrote two notes, in this form:

DEAR MADAM,—Your husband can make a large sum of money (and be entirely protected from the law) by making an immediate appointment with me.

Chief BLUNT.

He sent one of these by his confidential messenger to the "reputed wife" of Brick Duffy, and the other to the reputed wife of Red McFadden.

Within the hour these offensive answers came:

YE OWLD FOOL: brick Duffys bin ded 2 yere.

BRIDGET MAHONEY.

CHIEF BAT,—Red McFadden is hung and in heving 18 month. Any ass but a detective knose that.

MARY O'HOOLIGAN.

"I have long suspected these facts," said the inspector; "this testimony proves the unerring accuracy of my instinct."

The moment one resource failed him he was ready with another. He immediately wrote an advertisement for the morning papers, and I kept a copy of it:

A.—xwblv. 242 N. Tjnd—fz328wmlg. Ozpo,—; 2 m! ogw. Mum.

He said that if the thief was alive this would bring him to the usual rendezvous. He further explained that the usual rendezvous was a place where all business affairs between detectives and criminals were conducted. This meeting would take place at twelve the next night.

We could do nothing till then, and I lost no time in getting out of the office, and was grateful indeed for the privilege.

At eleven the next night I brought one hundred thousand dollars in bank-notes and put them into the chief's hands, and shortly afterward he took his leave, with the brave old undimmed confidence in his eye. An almost intolerable hour dragged to a close; then I heard his welcome tread, and rose gasping and tottered to meet him. How his fine eyes flamed with triumph! He said:

"We've compromised! The jokers will sing a different tune to-morrow! Follow me!"

He took a lighted candle and strode down into the vast vaulted basement where sixty detectives always slept, and where a score were now playing cards to while the time. I followed close after him. He walked swiftly down to the dim and remote end of the place, and just as I succumbed to the pangs of suffocation and was swooning away he stumbled and fell over the outlying members of a mighty object, and I heard him exclaim as he went down:

"Our noble profession is vindicated. Here is your elephant!"

I was carried to the office above and restored with carbolic acid. The whole detective force swarmed in, and such another season of triumphant rejoicing ensued as I had never witnessed before. The reporters were called, baskets of champagne were opened, toasts were drunk, the handshakings and congratulations were continuous and enthusiastic. Naturally the chief was the hero of the hour, and his happiness was so complete and had been so patiently and worthily and bravely won that it made me happy to see it, though I stood there a homeless beggar, my priceless charge dead, and my position in my country's service lost to me through what would always seem my fatally careless execution of a great trust. Many an eloquent eye testified its deep admiration for the chief, and many a detective's voice murmured, "Look at him—just the king of the profession: only give him a clue, it's all he wants, and there ain't anything hid that he can't find." The dividing of the fifty thousand dollars made great pleasure; when it was finished the chief made a little speech while he put his share in his pocket, in which he said, "Enjoy it, boys, for you've earned it; and, more than that, you've earned for the detective profession undying fame."

A telegram arrived, which read:

MONROE, MICH., 10 P.M.

First time I've struck a telegraph office in over three weeks. Have followed those footprints, horseback, through the woods, a thousand miles to here, and they get stronger and bigger and fresher every day. Don't worry—inside of another week I'll have the elephant. This is dead sure.

DARLEY, *Detective.*

The chief ordered three cheers for "Darley, one of the finest minds on the force," and then commanded that he be telegraphed to come home and receive his share of the reward.

So ended that marvelous episode of the stolen elephant. The newspapers were pleasant with praises once more, the next day, with one contemptible exception. This sheet said, "Great is the detective! He may be a little slow in finding a little thing like a mislaid elephant—he may hunt him all day and sleep with his rotting carcass all night for three weeks, but he will find him at last—if he can get the man who mislaid him to show him the place!"

Poor Hassan was lost to me forever. The cannon-shots had wounded him fatally, he had crept to that unfriendly place in the fog, and there, surrounded by his enemies and in constant danger of detection, he had wasted away with hunger and suffering till death gave him peace.

The compromise cost me one hundred thousand dollars; my detective expenses were forty-two thousand dollars more; I never applied for a place again under my government; I am a ruined man and a wanderer on the earth—but my admiration for that man, whom I believe to be the greatest detective the world has ever produced, remains undimmed to this day, and will so remain unto the end.

CORN-PONE OPINIONS

(Written in 1900)

FIFTY years ago, when I was a boy of fifteen and helping to inhabit a Missourian village on the banks of the Mississippi, I had a friend whose society was very dear to me because I was forbidden by my mother to partake of it. He was a gay and impudent and satirical and delightful young black man—a slave—who daily preached sermons from the top of his master's woodpile, with me for sole audience. He imitated the pulpit style of the several clergymen of the village, and did it well, and with fine passion and energy. To me he was a wonder. I believed he was the greatest orator in the United States and would some day be heard from. But it did not happen; in the distribution of rewards he was overlooked. It is the way, in this world.

He interrupted his preaching, now and then, to saw a stick of wood; but the sawing was a pretense—he did it with his mouth; exactly imitating the sound the bucksaw makes in shrieking its way through the wood. But it served its purpose; it kept his master from coming out to see how the work was getting along. I listened to the sermons from the open window of a lumber room at the back of the house. One of his texts was this:

"You tell me whar a man gits his corn pone, en I'll tell you what his 'pinions is."

I can never forget it. It was deeply impressed upon me. By my mother. Not upon my memory, but elsewhere. She had slipped in upon me while I was absorbed and not watching. The black philosopher's idea was that a man is not independent, and cannot afford views which might interfere with his bread and butter. If he would prosper, he must train with the majority; in matters of large moment, like politics and religion, he must think and feel with the bulk of his neighbors, or suffer damage in his social standing and in his business prosperities. He must restrict himself to corn-pone opinions—at least on the surface. He must get his opinions from other people; he must reason out none for himself; he must have no first-hand views.

I think Jerry was right, in the main, but I think he did not go far enough.

1. It was his idea that a man conforms to the majority view of his locality by calculation and intention.

This happens, but I think it is not the rule.

2. It was his idea that there is such a thing as a first-hand opinion; an original opinion; an opinion which is coldly reasoned out in a man's head, by a searching analysis of the facts involved, with the heart unconsulted, and the jury room closed against outside influences. It may be that such an opinion has been born somewhere, at some time or other, but I suppose it got away before they could catch it and stuff it and put it in the museum.

I am persuaded that a coldly-thought-out and independent verdict upon a fashion in clothes, or manners, or literature, or politics, or religion, or any other matter that is projected into the field of our notice and interest, is a most rare thing—if it has indeed ever existed.

A new thing in costume appears—the flaring hoopskirt, for example—and the passers-by are shocked, and the irreverent laugh. Six months later everybody is reconciled; the fashion has established itself; it is admired, now, and no one laughs. Public opinion resented it before, public opinion accepts it now, and is happy in it. Why? Was the resentment reasoned out? Was the acceptance reasoned out? No. The instinct that moves to conformity did the work. It is our nature to conform; it is a force which not many can successfully resist. What is its seat? The inborn requirement of self-approval. We all have to bow to that; there are no exceptions. Even the woman who refuses from first to last to wear the hoopskirt comes under that law and is its slave; she could not wear the skirt and have her own approval; and that she *must* have, she cannot help herself. But as a rule our self-approval has its source in but one place and not elsewhere—the approval of other people. A person of vast consequences can introduce any kind of novelty in dress and the general world will presently adopt it—moved to do it, in the first place, by the natural instinct to passively yield to that vague something recognized as authority, and in the second place by the human instinct to train with the multitude and have its approval. An empress introduced the hoopskirt, and we know the result. A nobody introduced the bloomer, and we know the result. If Eve should come again, in her ripe renown, and reintroduce her quaint styles—well, we know what would happen.

And we should be cruelly embarrassed, along at first.

The hoopskirt runs its course and disappears. Nobody reasons about it. One woman abandons the fashion; her neighbor notices this and follows her lead; this influences the next woman; and so on and so on, and presently the skirt has vanished out of the world, no one knows how nor why; nor cares, for that matter. It will come again, by and by; and in due course will go again.

Twenty-five years ago, in England, six or eight wine glasses stood grouped by each person's plate at a dinner party, and they were used, not left idle and empty; to-day there are but three or four in the group, and the average guest sparingly uses about two of them. We have not adopted this new fashion yet, but we shall do it presently. We shall not think it out; we shall merely conform, and let it go at that. We get our notions and habits and opinions from outside influences; we do not have to study them out.

Our table manners, and company manners, and street manners change from time to time, but the changes are not reasoned out; we merely notice and conform. We are creatures of outside influences; as a rule we do not think, we only imitate. We cannot invent standards that will stick; what we mistake for standards are only fashions, and perishable. We may continue to admire them, but we drop the use of them. We notice this in literature. Shakespeare is a standard, and fifty years ago we used to write tragedies which we couldn't tell from—from somebody's else; but we don't do it any more, now. Our prose standard, three quarters of a century ago, was ornate and diffuse; some authority or other changed it in the direction of compactness and simplicity, and conformity followed, without argument. The historical novel starts up suddenly, and sweeps the land. Everybody writes one, and the nation is glad. We had historical novels before; but nobody read them, and the rest of us conformed—without reasoning it out. We are conforming in the other way, now, because it is another case of everybody.

The outside influences are always pouring in upon us, and we are always obeying their orders and accepting their verdicts. The Smiths like the new play; the Joneses go to see it, and they copy the Smith verdict. Morals, religion, politics, get their following from surrounding influences and atmospheres, almost entirely; not from study, not from thinking. A man must and will have his own approval first of all, in each and every moment and circumstance of his life—even if he must repent of a self-approved act the moment after its commission, in order to get his self-approval again: but, speaking in general terms, a man's self-approval in the large concerns of life has its source in the approval of the peoples about him, and not in a searching personal examination of the matter. Mohammedans are Mohammedans because they are born and reared among that sect, not because they have thought it out and can furnish sound reasons for being Mohammedans; we know why Catholics are Catholics; why Presbyterians are Presbyterians; why Baptists are Baptists; why Mormons are Mormons; why thieves are thieves; why monarchists are monarchists; why Republicans are Republicans and Democrats, Democrats. We know it is a matter of association and sympathy, not reasoning and examination; that hardly a man in the world has an opinion upon morals, politics, or religion which he got otherwise than through his associations and sympathies. Broadly speaking, there are none but corn-pone opinions. And broadly speaking, corn-pone stands for self-approval. Self-approval is acquired mainly from the approval of other people. The result is conformity. Sometimes conformity has a sordid business interest—the bread-and-butter interest—but not in most cases, I think. I think that in the majority of cases it is unconscious and not calculated; that it is born of the human being's natural yearning to stand well with his fellows and have their inspiring approval and praise—a yearning which is commonly so strong and so insistent that it cannot be effectually resisted, and must have its way.

A political emergency brings out the corn-pone opinion in fine force in its two chief varieties—the pocketbook variety, which has its origin in self-interest, and the bigger variety, the sentimental variety—the one which can't bear to be outside the pale; can't bear to be in disfavor; can't endure the averted face and the cold shoulder; wants to stand well with his friends, wants to be smiled upon, wants to be welcome, wants to hear the precious words, "*He's* on the right track!" Uttered perhaps by an ass, but still an ass of high degree, an ass whose approval is gold and diamonds to a smaller ass, and confers glory and honor and happiness, and membership in the herd. For these gauds many a man will dump his life-long principles into the street, and his conscience along with them. We have seen it happen. In some millions of instances.

Men think they think upon great political questions, and they do; but they think with their party, not independently; they read its literature, but not that of the other side; they arrive at convictions, but they are drawn from a partial view of the matter in hand and are of no particular value. They swarm with their party, they feel with their party, they are happy in their party's approval; and where the party leads they will fol-follow, whether for right and honor, or through blood and dirt and a mush of mutilated morals.

In our late canvass half of the nation passionately believed that in silver lay salvation, the other half as passionately believed that that way lay destruction. Do you believe that a tenth part of the people, on either side, had any rational excuse for having an opinion about the matter at all? I studied that mighty question to the bottom—came out empty. Half of our people passionately believe in high tariff, the other half believe otherwise. Does this mean study and examination or only feeling? The latter, I think. I have deeply studied that question, too—and didn't arrive. We all do no end of feeling, and we mistake it for thinking. And out of it we get an aggregation which we consider a boon. Its name is Public Opinion. It is held in reverence. It settles everything. Some think it the Voice of God.

CHAPTER XIV

RANK AND DIGNITY OF PILOTING

IN my preceding chapters I have tried, by going into the minutiæ of the science of piloting, to carry the reader step by step to a comprehension of what the science consists of; and at the same time I have tried to show him that it is a very curious and wonderful science, too, and very worthy of his attention. If I have seemed to love my subject, it is no surprising thing, for I loved the profession far better than any I have followed since, and I took a measureless pride in it. The reason is plain: a pilot, in those days, was the only unfettered and entirely independent human being that lived in the earth. Kings are but the hampered servants of parliament and the people; parliaments sit in chains forged by their constituency; the editor of a newspaper cannot be independent, but must work with one hand tied behind him by party and patrons, and be content to utter only half or two-thirds of his mind; no clergyman is a free man and may speak the whole truth, regardless of his parish's opinions; writers of all kinds are manacled servants of the public. We write frankly and fearlessly, but then we "modify" before we print. In truth, every man and woman and child has a master, and worries and frets in servitude; but, in the day I write of, the Mississippi pilot had *none.* The captain could stand upon the hurricane-deck, in the pomp of a very brief authority, and give him five or six orders while the vessel backed into the stream, and then that skipper's reign was over. The moment that the boat was under way in the river, she was under the sole and unquestioned control of the pilot. He could do with her exactly as he pleased, run her when and whither he chose, and tie her up to the bank whenever his judgment said that that course was best. His movements were entirely free; he consulted no one, he received commands from nobody, he promptly resented even the merest suggestions. Indeed, the law of the United States forbade him to listen to commands or suggestions, rightly considering that the pilot necessarily knew better how to handle the boat than anybody could tell him. So here was the novelty of a king without a keeper, an absolute monarch who was absolute in sober truth and not by a fiction of words. I have seen a boy of eighteen taking a great steamer serenely into what seemed almost certain destruction, and the aged captain standing mutely by, filled with apprehension but powerless to interfere. His interference, in that particular instance, might have been an excellent thing, but to permit it would have been to establish a most pernicious precedent. It will easily be guessed, considering the pilot's boundless authority, that he was a great personage in the old steamboating days. He was treated with marked courtesy by the captain and with marked deference by all the officers and servants; and this deferential spirit was quickly communicated to the passengers, too. I think pilots were about the only people I ever knew who failed to show, in some degree, embarrassment in the presence of traveling foreign princes. But then, people in one's own grade of life are not usually embarrassing objects.

By long habit, pilots came to put all their wishes in the form of commands. It "gravels" me, to this day, to put my will in the weak shape of a request, instead of launching it in the crisp language of an order.

In those old days, to load a steamboat at St. Louis, take her to New Orleans and back, and discharge cargo, consumed about twenty-five days, on an average. Seven or eight of these days the boat spent at the wharves of St. Louis and New Orleans, and every soul on board was hard at work, except the two pilots; *they* did nothing but play gentleman up-town, and receive the same wages for it as if they had been on duty. The moment the boat touched the wharf at either city they were ashore; and they were not likely to be seen again till the last bell was ringing and everything in readiness for another voyage.

When a captain got hold of a pilot of particularly high reputation, he took pains to keep him. When wages were four hundred dollars a month on the Upper Mississippi, I have known a captain to keep such a pilot in idleness, under full pay, three months at a time, while the river was frozen up. And one must remember that in those cheap times four hundred dollars was a salary of almost inconceivable splendor. Few men on shore got such pay as that, and when they did they were mightily looked up to. When pilots from either end of the river wandered into our small Missouri village, they were sought by the best and the fairest, and treated with exalted respect. Lying in port under wages was a thing which many pilots greatly enjoyed and appreciated; especially if they belonged in the Missouri River in the heyday of that trade (Kansas times), and got nine hundred dollars a trip, which was equivalent to about eighteen hundred dollars a month. Here is a conversation of that day. A chap out of the Illinois River, with a little stern-wheel tub, accosts a couple of ornate and gilded Missouri River pilots:

"Gentlemen, I've got a pretty good trip for the up-country, and shall want you about a month. How much will it be?"

"Eighteen hundred dollars apiece."

"Heavens and earth! You take my boat, let me have your wages, and I'll divide!"

I will remark, in passing, that Mississippi steamboatmen were important in landsmen's eyes (and in their own, too, in a degree) according to the dignity of the boat they were on. For instance, it was a proud thing to be of the crew of such stately craft as the *Aleck Scott* or the *Grand Turk*. Negro firemen, deck-hands, and barbers belonging to those boats were distinguished personages in their grade of life and they were well aware of that fact, too. A stalwart darky once gave offense at a negro ball in New Orleans by putting on a good many airs. Finally one of the managers bustled up to him and said:

"Who *is* you, anyway? Who *is* you? dat's what *I* wants to know!"

The offender was not disconcerted in the least, but swelled himself up and threw that into his voice which showed that he knew he was not putting on all those airs on a stinted capital.

"Who *is* I? Who *is* I? I let you know mighty quick who I is! I want you niggers to understan' dat I fires de middle do'[1] on de *Aleck Scott!*

That was sufficient.

The barber of the *Grand Turk* was a spruce young negro, who aired his importance with balmy complacency, and was greatly courted by the circle in which he moved. The young colored population of New Orleans were much given to flirting, at twilight, on the banquettes of the back streets. Somebody saw and heard something like the following, one evening, in one of those localities. A middle-aged negro woman projected her head through a broken pane and shouted (very willing that the neighbors should hear and envy), "You Mary Ann, come in de

[1] Door

house dis minute! Stannin' out dah foolin' 'long wid dat low trash, an' heah's de barber off'n de *Gran' Turk* wants to converse wid you!"

My reference, a moment ago, to the fact that a pilot's peculiar official position placed him out of the reach of criticism or command, brings Stephen W. naturally to my mind. He was a gifted pilot, a good fellow, a tireless talker, and had both wit and humor in him. He had a most irreverent independence, too, and was deliciously easy-going and comfortable in the presence of age, official dignity, and even the most august wealth. He always had work, he never saved a penny, he was a most persuasive borrower, he was in debt to every pilot on the river, and to the majority of the captains. He could throw a sort of splendor around a bit of harum-scarum, devil-may-care piloting, that made it almost fascinating—but not to everybody. He made a trip with good old Captain Y. once, and was "relieved" from duty when the boat got to New Orleans. Somebody expressed surprise at the discharge. Captain Y., shuddered at the mere mention of Stephen. Then his poor, thin old voice piped out something like this:

"Why, bless me! I wouldn't have such a wild creature on my boat for the world—not for the whole world! He swears, he sings, he whistles, he yells—I never saw such an Injun to yell. All times of the night—it never made any difference to him. He would just yell that way, not for anything in particular, but merely on account of a kind of devilish comfort he got out of it. I never could get into a sound sleep but he would fetch me out of bed, all in a cold sweat, with one of those dreadful war-whoops. A queer being—very queer being; no respect for anything or anybody. Sometimes he called me 'Johnny.' And he kept a fiddle and a cat. He played execrably. This seemed to distress the cat, and so the cat would howl. Nobody could sleep where that man—and his family—was. And reckless? There never was anything like it. Now you may believe it or not, but as sure as I am sitting here, he brought my boat a-tilting down through those awful snags at Chicot under a rattling head of steam, and the wind a-blowing like the very nation, at that! My officers will tell you so. They saw it. And, sir, while he was a-tearing right down through those snags, and I a-shaking in my shoes and praying, I wish I may never speak again if he didn't pucker up his mouth and go to *whistling!* Yes, sir; whistling 'Buffalo gals, can't you come out to-night, can't you come out to-night, can't you come out to-night'; and doing it as calmly as if we were attending a funeral and weren't related to the corpse. And when I remonstrated with him about it, he smiled down on me as if I was his child, and told me to run in the house and try to be good, and not be meddling with my superiors!"[1]

Once a pretty mean captain caught Stephen in New Orleans out of work and as usual out of money. He laid steady siege to Stephen, who was in a very "close place," and finally persuaded him to hire with him at one hundred and twenty-five dollars per month, just half wages, the captain agreeing not to divulge the secret and so bring down the contempt of all the guild upon the poor fellow. But the boat was not more than a day out of New Orleans before Stephen discovered that the captain was boasting of his exploit, and that all the officers had been told. Stephen winced, but said nothing. About the middle of the afternoon the captain stepped out on the hurricane-deck, cast his eyes around, and looked a good deal surprised. He glanced inquiringly aloft at Stephen, but Stephen was whistling placidly and attending to business. The captain stood around awhile in evident discomfort, and once or twice semed about to make a suggestion; but the etiquette of the river taught him to avoid that sort of rashness, and so he managed to hold his peace. He chafed and puzzled a few minutes longer, then retired to his apartments. But soon he was out again, and apparently more perplexed than ever. Presently he ventured to remark, with deference:

"Pretty good stage of the river now, ain't it, sir?"

"Well, I should say so! Bank-full *is* a pretty liberal stage."

"Seems to be a good deal of current here."

"Good deal don't describe it! It's worse than a mill-race."

"Isn't it easier in toward shore than it is out here in the middle?"

"Yes, I reckon it is; but a body can't be too careful with a steamboat. It's pretty safe out here; can't strike any bottom here, you can depend on that."

The captain departed, looking rueful enough. At this rate, he would probably die of old age before his boat got to St. Louis. Next day he appeared on deck and again found Stephen faithfully standing up the middle of the river, fighting the whole

[1] Considering a captain's ostentatious but hollow chieftainship, and a pilot's real authority, there was something impudently apt and happy about that way of phrasing it.

vast force of the Mississippi, and whistling the same placid tune. This thing was becoming serious. In by the shore was a slower boat clipping along in the easy water and gaining steadily; she began to make for an island chute; Stephen stuck to the middle of the river. Speech was *wrung* from the captain. He said:

"Mr. W., don't that chute cut off a good deal of distance?"

"I think it does, but I don't know."

"Don't know! Well, isn't there water enough in it now to go through?"

"I expect there is, but I am not certain."

"Upon my word this is odd! Why, those pilots on that boat yonder are going to try it. Do you mean to say that you don't know as much as they do?"

"They! Why, *they* are two-hundred-and-fifty-dollar pilots! But don't you be uneasy; I know as much as any man can afford to know for a hundred and twenty-five!"

The captain surrendered.

Five minutes later Stephen was bowling through the chute and showing the rival boat a two-hundred-and-fifty-dollar pair of heels.

MY FIRST LIE, AND HOW I GOT OUT OF IT

AS I understand it, what you desire is information about "my first lie, and how I got out of it." I was born in 1835; I am well along, and my memory is not as good as it was. If you had asked about my first truth it would have been easier for me and kinder of you, for I remember that fairly well; I remember it as if it were last week. The family think it was week before, but that is flattery and probably has a selfish project back of it. When a person has become seasoned by experience and has reached the age of sixty-four, which is the age of discretion, he likes a family compliment as well as ever, but he does not lose his head over it as in the old innocent days.

I do not remember my first lie, it is too far back; but I remember my second one very well. I was nine days old at the time, and had noticed that if a pin was sticking in me and I advertised it in the usual fashion, I was lovingly petted and coddled and pitied in a most agreeable way and got a ration between meals besides. It was human nature to want to get these riches, and I fell. I lied about the pin—advertising one when there wasn't any. You would have done it; George Washington did it; anybody would have done it. During the first half of my life I never knew a child that was able to rise above that temptation and keep from telling that lie. Up to 1867 all the civilized children that were ever born into the world were liars—including George. Then the safety-pin came in and blocked the game. But is that reform worth anything? No; for it is reform by force and has no virtue in it; it merely stops that form of lying; it doesn't impair the disposition to lie, by a shade. It is the cradle application of conversion by fire and sword, or of the temperance principle through prohibition.

To return to that early lie. They found no pin, and they realized that another liar had been added to the world's supply. For by grace of a rare inspiration, a quite commonplace but seldom noticed fact was borne in upon their understandings—that almost all lies are acts, and speech has no part in them. Then, if they examined a little further they recognized that all people are liars from the cradle onward, without exception, and that they begin to lie as soon as they wake in the morning, and keep it up, without rest or refreshment, until they go to sleep at night. If they arrived at that truth it probably grieved them—did, if they had been heedlessly and ignorantly educated by their books and teachers; for why should a person grieve over a thing which by the eternal law of his make he cannot help? He didn't invent the law; it is merely his business to obey it and keep still; join the universal conspiracy and keep so still that he shall deceive his fellow-conspirators into imagining that he doesn't know that the law exists. It is what we all do—we that know. I am speaking of the lie of silent assertion; we can tell it without saying a word, and we all do it—we that know. In the magnitude of its territorial spread it is one of the most majestic lies that the civilizations make it their sacred and anxious care to guard and watch and propagate.

For instance: It would not be possible for a humane and intelligent person to invent a rational excuse for slavery; yet you will remember that in the early days of the emancipation agitation in the North, the agitators got but small help or countenance from any one. Argue and plead and pray as they might, they could not break the universal stillness that reigned, from pulpit and press all the way down to the bottom of society—the clammy stillness created and maintained by the lie of silent assertion—the silent assertion that there wasn't anything going on in which humane and intelligent people were interested.

From the beginning of the Dreyfus case to the end of it, all France, except a couple of dozen moral paladins, lay under the smother of the silent-assertion lie that no wrong was being done to a persecuted and unoffending man. The like smother was over England lately, a good half of the population silently letting on that they were not aware that Mr. Chamberlain was trying to manufacture a war in South Africa and was willing to pay fancy prices for the materials.

Now there we have instances of three prominent ostensible civilizations working the silent-assertion lie. Could one find other instances in the three countries? I think so. Not so very many, perhaps, but say a billion—just so as to keep within bounds. Are those countries working that kind of lie, day in and day out, in thousands and thousands of varieties, without ever resting? Yes, we know that to be true. The universal conspiracy of the silent-assertion lie is hard at work always and everywhere, and always in the interest of a stupidity or a sham, never in the interest of a thing fine or respectable. Is it the most timid and shabby of all lies? It seems to have the look of it. For ages and ages it has mutely labored in the interest of despotisms and aristocracies and chattel slaveries, and military slaveries, and religious slaveries, and has kept them alive; keeps them alive yet, here and there and yonder, all about the globe; and will go on keeping them alive until the silent-assertion lie retires from business—the silent assertion that nothing is going on which fair and intelligent men are aware of and are engaged by their duty to try to stop.

What I am arriving at is this: When whole races and peoples conspire to propagate gigantic mute lies in the interest of tyrannies and shams, why should we care anything about the trifling lies told by individuals? Why should we try to make it appear that abstention from lying is a virtue? Why should we want to beguile ourselves in that way? Why should we without shame help the nation lie, and then be ashamed to do a little lying on our own account? Why should't we be honest and honorable, and lie every time we get a chance? That is to say, why shouldn't we be consistent, and either lie all the time or not at all? Why should we help the nation lie the whole day long and then object to telling one little individual private lie in our own interest to go to bed on? Just for the refreshment of it, I mean, and to take the rancid taste out of our mouth.

Here in England they have the oddest ways. Thy won't tell a spoken lie—nothing can persuade them. Except in a large moral interest, like politics or religion, I mean. To tell a spoken lie to get even the poorest little personal advantage out of it is a thing which is impossible to them. They make me ashamed of myself sometimes, they are so bigoted. They will not even tell a lie for the fun of it; they will not tell it when it hasn't even a suggestion of damage or advantage in it for any one. This has a restraining influence upon me in spite of reason, and I am always getting out of practice.

Of course, they tell all sorts of little unspoken lies, just like anybody; but they don't notice it until their attention is called to it. They have got me so that sometimes I never tell a verbal lie now except in a modified form; and even in the modified form they don't approve of it. Still, that is as far as I can go in the interest of the growing friendly relations between the two countries; I must keep some of my self-respect—and my health. I can live on a low diet, but I can't get along on no sustenance at all.

Of course, there are times when these people have to come out with a spoken lie, for that is a thing which happens to everybody once in a while, and would happen to the angels if they came down here much. Particularly to the angels, in fact, for the lies I speak of are self-sacrificing ones told for a generous object, not a mean one; but even when these people tell a lie of that sort it seems to scare them and unsettle their minds. It is a wonderful thing to see, and shows that they are all insane. In fact, it is a country full of the most interesting superstitions.

I have an English friend of twenty-five years' standing, and yesterday when we were coming downtown on top of the bus I happened to tell him a lie—a modified one, of course; a half-breed, a mulatto: I can't seem to tell any other kind now, the market is so flat. I was explaining to him how I got out of an embarrassment in Austria last year. I do not know what might have become of me if I hadn't happened to remember to tell the police that I belonged to the same family as the Prince of Wales. That made everything pleasant, and they let me go; and apologized, too, and were ever so kind and obliging and polite, and couldn't do too much for me, and explained how the mistake came to be made, and promised to hang the officer that did it, and hoped I would let bygones be bygones and not say anything about it; and I said they could depend on me. My friend said, austerely:

"You call it a modified lie? Where is the modification?"

I explained that it lay in the form of my statement to the police.

"I didn't say I belonged to the royal family: I only said I belonged to the same family as the Prince—meaning the human family, of course; and if those people had had any penetration they would have known it. I can't go around furnishing brains to the police; it is not to be expected."

"How did you feel after that performance?"

"Well, of course I was distressed to find that the police had misunderstood me, but as long as I had not told any lie I knew there was no occasion to sit up nights and worry about it."

My friend struggled with the case several minutes, turning it over and examining it in his mind; then he said that so far as he could see the modification was itself a lie, being a misleading reservation of an explanatory fact; so I had told two lies instead of one.

"I wouldn't have done it," said he: "I have never told a lie, and I should be very sorry to do such a thing."

Just then he lifted his hat and smiled a basketful of surprised and delightful smiles down at a gentleman who was passing in a hansom.

"Who was that, G——?"

"I don't know."

"Then why did you do that?"

"Because I saw he thought he knew me and was expecting it of me. If I hadn't done it he would have been hurt. I didn't want to embarrass him before the whole street."

"Well, your heart was right, G——, and your act was right. What you did was kindly and courteous and beautiful; I would have done it myself: but it was a lie."

"A lie?" I didn't say a word. How do you make it out?"

"I know you didn't speak, still you said to him very plainly and enthusiastically in dumb show, 'Hello! you in town? Awful glad to see you, old fellow; when did you get back?' Concealed in your actions was what you have called 'a misleading reservation of an explanatory fact'—the fact that you had never seen him before. You expressed joy in encountering him—a lie; and you made that reservation—another lie. It was my pair over again. But don't be troubled—we all do it."

Two hours later, at dinner, when quite other matters were being discussed, he told how he happened along once just in the nick of time to do a great service for a family who were old friends of his. The head of it had suddenly died in circumstances and surroundings of a ruinously disgraceful character. If known, the facts would break the hearts of the innocent family and put upon them a load of unendurable shame. There was no help but in a giant lie, and he girded up his loins and told it.

"The family never found out, G——?"

"Never. In all these years they have never suspected. They were proud of him, and always had reason to be; they are proud of him yet, and to them his memory is sacred and stainless and beautiful."

"They had a narrow escape, G——."

"Indeed they had."

"For the very next man that came along might have been one of these heartless and shameless truthmongers. You have told the truth a million times in your life, G——, but that one golden lie atones for it all. Persevere."

Some may think me not strict enough in my morals, but that position is hardly tenable. There are many kinds of lying which

I do not approve. I do not like an injurious lie, except when it injures somebody else; and I do not like the lie of bravado, nor the lie of virtuous ecstasy: the latter was affected by Bryant, the former by Carlyle.

Mr. Bryant said, "Truth crushed to earth will rise again."

I have taken medals at thirteen world's fairs, and may claim to be not without capacity, but I never told as big a one as that which Mr. Bryant was playing to the gallery; we all do it. Carlyle said, in substance, this—I do not remember the exact words: "This gospel is eternal—that a lie shall not live."

I have a reverent affection for Carlyle's books, and have read his *Revolution* eight times; and so I prefer to think he was not entirely at himself when he told that one. To me it is plain that he said it in a moment of excitement, when chasing Americans out of his back yard with brickbats. They used to go there and worship. At bottom he was probably fond of them, but he was always able to conceal it. He kept bricks for them, but he was not a good shot, and it is matter of history that when he fired they dodged, and carried off the brick; for as a nation we like relics, and so long as we get them we do not much care what the reliquary thinks obout it. I am quite sure that when he told that large one about a lie not being able to live, he had just missed an American and was over-excited. He told it above thirty years ago, but it is alive yet; alive, and very healthy and hearty, and likely to outlive any fact in history. Carlyle was truthful when calm, but give him Americans enough and bricks enough and he could have taken medals himself.

As regards that time that George Washington told the truth, a word must be said, of course. It is the principal jewel in the crown of America, and it is but natural that we should work for all it is worth, as Milton says in his "Lay of the Last Minstrel." It was a timely and judicious truth, and I should have told it myself in the circumstances. But I should have stopped there. It was a stately truth, a lofty truth—a Tower; and I think it was a mistake to go on and distract attention from its sublimity by building another Tower alongside of it fourteen times as high. I refer to his remark that he "could not lie." I should have fed that to the marines: or left it to Carlyle; it is just in his style. It would have taken a medal at any European fair, and would have got an Honorable Mention even at Chicago if it had been saved up. But let it pass: the Father of his Country was excited. I have been in those circumstances, and I recollect.

With the truth he told I have no objection to offer, as already indicated. I think it was not premeditated, but an inspiration. With his fine military mind, he had probably arranged to let his brother Edward in for the cherry-tree results, but by an inspiration he saw his opportunity in time and took advantage of it. By telling the truth he could astonish his father; his father would tell the neighbors; the neighbors would spread it; it would travel to all firesides; in the end it would make him President, and not only that, but First President. He was a far-seeing boy and would be likely to think of these things. Therefore, to my mind, he stands justified for what he did. But not for the other Tower: it was a mistake. Still, I don't know about that; upon reflection I think perhaps it wasn't. For indeed it is that Tower that makes the other one live. If he hadn't said "I cannot tell a lie," there would have been no convulsion. That was the earthquake that rocked the planet. That is the kind of statement that lives forever, and a fact barnacled to it has a good chance to share its immortality.

To sum up, on the whole I am satisfied with things the way they are. There is a prejudice against the spoken lie, but none against any other, and by examination and mathematical computation I find that the proportion of the spoken lie to the other varieties is as 1 to 22,894. Therefore the spoken lie is of no consequence, and it is not worth while to go around fussing about it and trying to make believe it is an important matter. The silent colossal National Lie that is the support and confederate of all the tyrannies and shams and inequalities and unfairnesses that afflict the peoples—that is the one to throw bricks and sermons at. But let us be judicious and let somebody else begin.

And then— But I have wandered from my text. How did I get out of my second lie? I think I got out with honor, but I cannot be sure, for it was a long time ago and some of the details have faded out of my memory. I recollect that I was reversed and stretched across some one's knee, and that something happened, but I cannot now remember what it was. I think there was music; but it is all dim now and blurred by the lapse of time, and this may be only a senile fancy.

MORE MAXIMS OF PUDD'NHEAD WILSON

From FOLLOWING THE EQUATOR[1]

These wisdoms are for the luring of youth toward high moral attitudes. The author did not gather them from practice, but from observation. To be good is noble; but to show others how to be good is nobler and no trouble.

A man may have no bad habits and have worse.

When in doubt, tell the truth.

It is more trouble to make a maxim than it is to do right.

A dozen direct censures are easier to bear than one morganatic[2] compliment.

Noise proves nothing. Often a hen who has merely laid an egg cackles as if she had laid an asteroid.

He was as shy as a newspaper is when referring to its own merits.

Truth is the most valuable thing we have. Let us economize it.

It could probably be shown by facts and figures that there is no dintinctly native American criminal class except Congress.

It is your human environment that makes climate.

Everything human is pathetic. The secret source of Humor itself is not joy but sorrow. There is no humor in heaven.

We should be careful to get out of an experience only the wisdom that is in it—and stop there; lest we be like the cat that sits down on a hot stove-lid. She will never sit down on a hot stove-lid again—and that is well; but also she will never sit down on a cold one any more.

[2] A special kind of marriage (see Webster), sometimes called "left-handed."

There are those who scoff at the schoolboy, calling him frivolous and shallow. Yet it was the schoolboy who said, "Faith is believing what you know ain't so."

The timid man yearns for full value and demands a tenth. A bold man strikes for double value and compromises on par.

We can secure other people's approval, if we do right and try hard; but our own is worth a hundred of it, and no way has been found out of securing that.

Truth is stranger than fiction—to some people, but I am measurably familiar with it.

Truth *is* stranger than fiction, but it is because Fiction is obliged to stick to possibilities; Truth isn't.

There is a Moral Sense, and there is an Immoral Sense. History shows us that the Moral Sense enables us to perceive morality and how to avoid it, and that the Immoral Sense enables us to perceive immorality and how to enjoy it.

The English are mentioned in the Bible: Blessed are the meek, for they shall inherit the earth.

It is easier to stay out than get out.

Pity is for the living, envy is for the dead.

It is by the goodness of God that in our country we have those three unspeakably precious things: freedom of speech, freedom of conscience, and the prudence never to practice either of them.

Man will do many things to get himself loved, he will do all things to get himself envied.

Nothing is so ignorant as a man's left hand, except a lady's watch.

Be careless in your dress if you must, but keep a tidy soul.

There is no such thing as "the Queen's English." The property has gone into the hands of a joint stock company and we own the bulk of the shares!

"Classic." A book which people praise and don't read.

There are people who can do all fine and heroic things but one! keep from telling their happiness to the unhappy.

Man is the Only Animal that Blushes. Or needs to.

The universal brotherhood of man is our most precious possession, what there is of it.

Let us be thankful for the fools. But for them the rest of us could not succeed.

When people do not respect us we are sharply offended; yet deep down in his private heart no man much respects himself.

Nature makes the locust with an appetite for crops; man would have made him with an appetite for sand.

The spirit of wrath—not the words—is the sin; and the spirit of wrath is cursing. We begin to swear before we can talk.

The man with a new idea is a Crank until the idea succeeds.

Let us be grateful to Adam our benefactor. He cut us out of the "blessing" of idleness and won for us the "curse" of labor.

Let us not be too particular. It is better to have old second-hand diamonds than none at all.

The Autocrat of Russia possesses more power than any other man in the earth; but he cannot stop a sneeze.

There are several good protections against temptations, but the surest is cowardice.

Names are not always what they seem. The common Welsh name Bzjxxllwcp is pronounced Jackson.

To succeed in the other trades, capacity must be shown; in the law, concealment of it will do.

Prosperity is the best protector of principle.

By trying we can easily learn to endure adversity. Another man's, I mean.

Few of us can stand prosperity. Another man's, I mean.

There is an old-time toast which is golden for its beauty. "When you ascend the hill of prosperity may you not meet a friend."

Each person is born to one possession which outvalues all his others—his last breath.

Hunger is the handmaid of genius.

The old saw says, "Let a sleeping dog lie." Right. Still, when there is much at stake it is better to get a newspaper to do it.

It takes your enemy and your friend, working together, to hurt you to the heart; the one to slander you and the other to get the news to you.

If the desire to kill and the opportunity to kill came always together, who would escape hanging?

Grief can take care of itself; but to get the full value of a joy you must have somebody to divide it with.

He had had much experience of physicians, and said, "The only way to keep your health is to eat what you don't want, drink what you don't like, and do what you'd druther not."

The man who is ostentatious of his modesty is twin to the statue that wears a fig-leaf.

Let me make the superstitions of a nation and I care not who makes its laws or its songs either.

Wrinkles should merely indicate where smiles have been.

True irreverence is disrespect for another man's god.

Do not undervalue the headache. While it is at its sharpest it seems a bad investment; but when relief begins, the unexpired remainder is worth $4 a minute.

There are 869 different forms of lying, but only one of them has been squarely forbidden. Thou shalt not bear false witness against thy neighbor.

There are two times in a man's life when he should not speculate: when he can't afford it, and when he can.

She was not quite what you would call refined. She was not quite what you would call unrefined. She was the kind of person that keeps a parrot.

Make it a point to do something every day that you don't want to do. This is the golden rule for acquiring the habit of doing your duty without pain.

Don't part with your illusions. When they are gone you may still exist but you have ceased to live.

Often, the surest way to convey misinformation is to tell the strict truth.

Satan (impatiently) to Newcomer: The trouble with you Chicago people is, that you think you are the best people down here; whereas you are merely the most numerous.

There are no people who are quite so vulgar as the over-refined ones.

The principal difference between a cat and a lie is that the cat has only nine lives.

When your watch gets out of order you have choice of two things to do: throw it in the fire or take it to the watch-tinker. The former is the quickest.

In statesmanship get the formalities right, never mind about the moralities.

Every one is a moon, and has a dark side which he never shows to anybody.

First catch your Boer,[1] then kick him.

None of us can have as many virtues as the fountain-pen, or half its cussedness; but we can try.

The very ink with which all history is written is merely fluid prejudice.

There isn't a Parallel of Latitude but thinks it would have been the Equator if it had had its rights.

I have traveled more than any one else, and I have noticed that even the angels speak English with an accent.

[1] At the time this was written England was having its troubles in defeating the Boers.

ON THE LADIES

From Mark Twain's Speeches

At the anniversary festival of the Scottish Corporation of London on Monday evening, in response to the toast of "The Ladies," Mark Twain spoke as follows:

I am proud, indeed, of the distinction of being chosen to respond to this especial toast, to 'The Ladies,' or to women if you please, for that is the preferable term, perhaps; it is certainly the older, and therefore the more entitled to reverence. [Laughter.] I have noticed that the Bible, with that plain, blunt honesty which is such a conspicuous characteristic of the Scriptures, is always particular to never refer to even the illustrious mother of all mankind herself as a 'lady,' but speaks of her as a woman. [Laughter.] It is odd, but you will find it is so. I am peculiarly proud of this honor, because I think that the toast to women is one which, by right and by every rule of gallantry, should take precedence of all others—of the army, of the navy, of even royalty itself—perhaps, though the latter is not necessary in this day and in this land, for the reason that, tacitly, you do drink a broad general health to all good women when you drink the health of the Queen of England and the Princess of Wales. [Loud cheers.] I have in mind a poem just now which is familiar to you all, familiar to everybody. And what an inspiration that was (and how instantly the present toast recalls the verses to all our minds) when the most noble, the most gracious, the purest, and sweetest of all poets says:

"Woman! O woman!—er—
Wom—"

[Laughter.] However, you remember the lines; and you remember how feelingly, how daintily, how almost imperceptibly the verses raise up before you, feature by feature, the ideal of a true and perfect woman; and how, as you contemplate the finished marvel, your homage grows into worship of the intellect that could create so fair a thing out of mere breath, mere words. And you call to mind now, as I speak, how the poet, with stern fidelity to the history of all humanity, delivers this beautiful child of his heart and his brain over to the trials and sorrows that must come to all, sooner or later, that abide in the earth, and how the pathetic story culminates in that apostrophe—so wild, so regretful, so full of mournful retrospection. The lines run thus:

"Alas! —alas!—a—alas!
——Alas!————alas!"

—and so on. [Laughter.] I do not remember the rest; but, taken together, it seems to me that poem is the noblest tribute to woman that human genius has ever brought forth—[laughter]—and I feel that if I were to talk hours I could not do my great theme completer or more graceful justice than I have now done in simply quoting that poet's matchless words. [Renewed laughter.] The phases of the womanly nature are infinite in their variety. Take any type of woman, and you shall find in it something to respect, something to admire, something to love. And you shall find the whole joining you heart and hand. Who was more patriotic than Joan of Arc? Who was braver? Who has given us a grander instance of self-sacrificing devotion? Ah! you remember, you remember well, what a throb of pain, what a great tidal wave of grief swept over us all when Joan of Arc fell at Waterloo. [Much laughter.] Who does not sorrow for the loss of Sappho, the sweet singer of Israel? [Laughter.] Who among us does not miss the gentle ministrations, the softening influences, the humble piety of Lucretia Borgia? [Laughter.] Who can join in the heartless libel that says woman is extravagant in dress when he can look back and call to mind our simple and lowly mother Eve arrayed in her modification of the Highland costume. [Roars of laughter.] Sir, women have been soldiers, women have been painters, women have been poets. As long as language lives the name of Cleopatra will live. And, not because she conquered George III.—[laughter]—but because she wrote those divine lines:—

"Let dogs delight to bark and bite,
For God hath made them so."

[More laughter.] The story of the world is adorned with the names of illustrious ones of our own sex—some of them sons of St. Andrew, too—Scott, Bruce, Burns, the warrior Wallace, Ben Nevis—[laughter]—the gifted Ben Lomond, and the great new Scotchman, Ben Disraeli.[1] [Great laughter.] Out of the

[1] Mr. Benjamin Disraeli, at that time Prime Minister of England, had just been elected Lord Rector of Glasgow University, and had made a speech which gave rise to a world of discussion. Ben Nevis and Ben Lomond are mountains in Scotland.

great plains of history tower whole mountain ranges of sublime women—the Queen of Sheba, Josephine, Semiramis, Sairey Gamp;[2] the list is endless—[laughter]—but I will not call the mighty roll, the names rise up in your own memories at the mere suggestion, luminous with the glory of deeds that cannot die, hallowed by the loving worship of the good and the true of all epochs and all climes. [Cheers.] Suffice it for our pride and our honor that we in our day have added to it such names as those of Grace Darling and Florence Nightingale. [Cheers.] Woman is all that she should be—gentle, patient, long suffering, trustful, unselfish, full of generous impulses. It is her blessed mission to comfort the sorrowing, plead for the erring, encourage the faint of purpose, succor the distressed, uplift the fallen, befriend the friendless—in a word, afford the healing of her sympathies and a home in her heart for all the bruised and persecuted children of misfortune that knock at its hospitable door. [Cheers.] And when I say, God bless her, there is none among us who has known the ennobling affection of a wife, or the steadfast devotion of a mother, but in his heart will say, Amen! [Loud and prolonged cheering.]

[2] A character not in history, but in Dickens.

SEVENTIETH BIRTHDAY

Address at a Dinner Given by Colonel George Harvey at Delmonico's, December 5, 1905, to Celebrate the Seventieth Anniversary of Mr. Clemens' Birth

Mr. Howells introduced Mr. Clemens:

"Now, ladies and gentlemen, and Colonel Harvey, I will try not to be greedy on your behalf in wishing the health of our honored and, in view of his great age, our revered guest. I will not say, 'Oh King, live forever!' but 'Oh King, live as long as you like!'" [Amid great applause and waving of napkins all rise and drink to Mark Twain.]

WELL, if I made that joke, it is the best one I ever made, and it is in the prettiest language, too. I never can get quite to that height. But I appreciate that joke, and I shall remember it—and I shall use it when occasion requires.

I have had a great many birthdays in my time. I remember the first one very well, and I always think of it with indignation; everything was so crude, unæsthetic, primeval. Nothing like this at all. No proper appreciative preparation made; nothing really ready. Now, for a person born with high and delicate instincts—why, even the cradle wasn't whitewashed—nothing ready at all. I hadn't any hair, I hadn't any teeth, I hadn't any clothes, I had to go to my first banquet just like that. Well, everybody came swarming in. It was the merest little bit of a village—hardly that, just a little hamlet, in the backwoods of Missouri, where nothing ever happened, and the people were all interested, and they all came; they looked me over to see if there was anything fresh in my line. Why, nothing ever happened in that village—I—why, I was the only thing that had really happened there for months and months and months; and although I say it myself that shouldn't, I came the nearest to being a real event that had happened in that village in more than two years. Well, those people came, they came with that curiosity which is so provincial, with that frankness which also is so provincial, and they examined me all around and gave their opinion. Nobody asked them, and I shouldn't have minded if anybody had paid me a compliment, but nobody did. Their opinions were all just green with prejudice, and I feel those opinions to this day. Well, I stood that as long as—well, you know I was born courteous, and I stood it to the limit. I stood it an hour, and then the worm turned. I was the worm; it was my turn to turn, and I turned. I knew very well the strength of my position; I knew that I was the only spotlessly pure and innocent person in that whole town, and I came out and said so. And they could not say a word. It was so true. They blushed; they were embarassed. Well, that was the first after-dinner speech I ever made. I think it was after dinner.

It's a long stretch between that first birthday speech and this one. That was my cradle-song, and this is my swan-song, I suppose. I am used to swan-songs; I have sung them several times.

This is my seventieth birthday, and I wonder if you all rise to the size of that proposition, realizing all the significance of that phrase, seventieth birthday.

The seventieth birthday! It is the time of life when you arrive at a new and awful dignity; when you may throw aside the decent reserves which have oppressed you for a generation and stand unafraid and unabashed upon your seven-terraced summit and look down and teach—unrebuked. You can tell the world how you got there. It is what they all do. You shall never get tired of telling by what delicate arts and deep moralities you climbed up to that great place. You will explain the process and dwell on the particulars with senile rapture. I have been anxious to explain my own system this long time, and now at last I have the right.

I have achieved my seventy years in the usual way: by sticking strictly to a scheme of life which would kill anybody else. It sounds like an exaggeration, but that is really the common rule for attaining to old age. When we examine the programme of any of these garrulous old people we always find that the habits which have preserved them would have decayed us; that the way of life which enabled them to live upon the property of their heirs so long, as Mr. Choate says, would have put us out of commission ahead of time. I will offer here, as a sound maxim, this: That we can't reach old age by another man's road.

I will now teach, offering my way of life to whomsoever desires to commit suicide by the scheme which has enabled me to beat the doctor and the hangman for seventy years. Some of the details may sound untrue, but they are not. I am not here to deceive; I am here to teach.

We have no permanent habits until we are forty. Then they begin to harden, presently they petrify, then business begins. Since forty I have been regular about going to bed and getting up—and that is one of the main things. I have made it a rule to go to bed when there wasn't anybody left to sit up with; and I have made it a rule to get up when I had to. This has resulted in an unswerving regularity of irregularity. It has saved me sound, but it would injure another person.

In the matter of diet—which is another main thing—I have been persistently strict in sticking to the things which didn't agree with me until one or the other of us got the best of it. Until lately I got the best of it myself. But last spring I stopped frolicking with mince-pie after midnight; up to then I had always believed it wasn't loaded. For thirty years I have taken coffee and bread at eight in the morning, and no bite nor sup until seven-thirty in the evening. Eleven hours. That is all right for me, and is wholesome, because I have never had a headache in my life, but headachy people would not reach seventy comfortably by that road, and they would be foolish to try it. And I wish to urge upon you this—which I think is wisdom—that if you find you can't make seventy by any but an uncomfortable road, don't you go. When they take off the Pullman and retire you to the rancid smoker, put on your things, count your checks, and get out at the first way station where there's a cemetery.

I have made it a rule never to smoke more than one cigar at a time. I have no other restriction as regards smoking. I do not know just when I began to smoke, I only know that it was in my father's lifetime, and that I was discreet. He passed from this life early in 1847, when I was a shade past eleven; ever since then I have smoked publicly. As an example to others, and not that I care for moderation myself, it has always been my rule never to smoke when asleep, and never to refrain when awake. It is a good rule. I mean, for me; but some of you know quite well that it wouldn't answer for everybody that's trying to get to be seventy.

I smoke in bed until I have to go to sleep; I wake up in the night, sometimes once, sometimes twice, sometimes three times, and I never waste any of these opportunities to smoke. This habit is so old and dear and precious to me that I would feel as you, sir, would feel if you should lose the only moral you've got—meaning the chairman—if you've got one: I am making no charges. I will grant, here, that I have stopped smoking now and then, for a few months at a time, but it was not on principle, it was only to show off; it was to pulverize those critics who said I was a slave to my habits and couldn't break my bonds.

Today it is all of sixty years since I began to smoke the limit. I have never bought cigars with life-belts around them. I early found that those were too expensive for me. I have always bought cheap cigars—reasonably cheap, at any rate. Sixty years ago they cost me four dollars a barrel, but my taste has improved, latterly, and I pay seven now. Six or seven. Seven, I think. Yes, its seven. But that includes the barrel. I often have smoking-parties at my house; but the people that come have always just taken the pledge. I wonder why that is?

As for drinking, I have no rule about that. When the others drink I like to help; otherwise I remain dry, by habit and preference. This dryness does not hurt me, but it could easily hurt you, because you are different. You let it alone.

Since I was seven years old I have seldom taken a dose of medicine, and have still seldomer needed one. But up to seven I lived exclusively on allopathic medicines. Not that I needed them, for I don't think I did; it was for economy; my father took a drug-store for a debt, and it made cod-liver oil cheaper than the other breakfast foods. We had nine barrels of it, and it lasted me seven years. Then I was weaned. The rest of the family had to get along with rhubarb and ipecac and such things, because I was the pet. I was the first Standard Oil Trust. I had it all. By the time the drug-store was exhausted my health was established, and there has never been much the matter with me since. But you know very well it would be foolish for the average child to start for seventy on that basis. It happened to be just the thing for me, but that was merely an accident; it couldn't happen again in a century.

I have never taken any exercise, except sleeping and resting, and I never intend to take any. Exercise is loathsome. And it cannot be any benefit when you are tired; and I was always tired. But let another person try my way, and see where he will come out.

I desire now to repeat and emphasize that maxim: We can't reach old age by another man's road. My habits protect my life, but they would assassinate you.

I have lived a severely moral life. But it would be a mistake for other people to try that, or for me to recommend it. Very few would succeed: you have to have a perfectly colossal stock of morals; and you can't get them on a margin; you have to have the whole thing, and put them in your box. Morals are an acquirement—like music, like a foreign language, like piety, poker, paralysis—no man is born with them. I wasn't myself, I started poor. I hadn't a single moral. There is hardly a man in this house that is poorer than I was then. Yes, I started like that—the world before me, not a moral in the slot. Not even an insurance moral. I can remember the first one I ever got. I can remember the landscape, the weather, the—I can remember how everything looked. It was an old moral, an old secondhand moral, all out of repair, and didn't fit, anyway. But if you are careful with a thing like that, and keep it in a dry place, and save it for processions, and Chautauquas, and World's Fairs, and so on, and disinfect it now and them, and give it a fresh coat of whitewash once in a while, you will be surprised to see how well she will last and how long she will keep sweet, or at least inoffensive. When I got that mouldy old moral, she had stopped growing, because she hadn't any exercise; but I worked her hard, I worked her Sundays and all. Under this cultivation she waxed in might and stature beyond belief, and served me well and was my pride and joy for sixty-three years; then she got to associating with insurance presidents, and lost flesh and character, and was a sorrow to look at and no longer competent for business. She was a great loss to me. Yet not all loss. I sold her—ah, pathetic skeleton, as she was—I sold her to Leopold, the pirate King of Belgium; he sold her to our Metropolitan Museum, and it was very glad to get her, for without a rag on, she stands 57 feet long and 16 feet high, and they think she's a brontosaur. Well, she looks it. They believe it will take nineteen geological periods to breed her match.

Morals are of inestimable value, for every man is born crammed with sin microbes, and the only thing that can extirpate these sin microbes is morals. Now you take a sterilized Christian—I mean, you take *the* sterilized Christian, for there's only one. Dear sir, I wish you wouldn't look at me like that.

Threescore years and ten!

It is the Scriptural statute of limitations. After that, you owe no active duties; for you the strenuous life is over. You are a time-expired man, to use Kipling's military phrase: You have served your term, well or less well, and you are mustered out. You are become an honorary member of the republic, you are emancipated, compulsions are not for you, nor any bugle-call but "lights out." You pay the time-worn duty bills if you choose, or decline if you prefer—and without prejudice—for they are not legally collectable.

The previous-engagement plea, which in forty years has cost you so many twinges, you can lay aside forever; on this side of the grave you will never need it again. If you shrink at thought of night, and winter, and the late home-coming from the banquet and the lights and the laughter through the deserted streets—a desolation which would not remind you now, as for a generation it did, that your friends are sleeping, and you must creep in a-tiptoe and not disturb them, but would only remind you that you need not tiptoe, you can never disturb them more—if you shrink at thought of these things, you need only reply, "Your invitation honors me, and pleases me because you still keep me in your remembrance, but I am seventy; seventy, and would nestle in the chimney-corner, and smoke my pipe, and read my book, and take my rest, wishing you well in all affection, and that when you in your return shall arrive at pier No. 70 you may step aboard your waiting ship with a reconciled spirit, and lay your course toward the sinking sun with a contented heart.

A CURIOUS DREAM[1]

CONTAINING A MORAL

NIGHT before last I had a singular dream. I seemed to be sitting on a doorstep (in no particular city perhaps) ruminating, and the time of night appeared to be about twelve or one o'clock. The weather was balmy and delicious. There was no human sound in the air, not even a footstep. There was no sound of any kind to emphasize the dead stillness, except the occasional hollow barking of a dog in the distance and the fainter answer of a further dog. Presently up the street I heard a bony clack-clacking, and guessed it was the castanets of a serenading party. In a minute more a tall skeleton, hooded, and half clad in a tattered and moldy shroud, whose shreds were flapping about the ribby latticework of its person, swung by me with a stately stride and disappeared in the gray gloom of the starlight. It had a broken and worm-eaten coffin on its shoulder and a bundle of something in its hand. I knew what the clack-clacking was then; it was this party's joints working together, and his elbows knocking against his sides as he walked. I may say I was surprised. Before I could collect my thoughts and enter upon any speculations as to what this apparition might portend, I heard another one coming—for I recognized his clack-clack. He had two-thirds of a coffin on his shoulder, and some foot and head boards under his arm. I mightily wanted to peer under his hood and speak to him, but when he turned and smiled upon me with his cavernous sockets and his projecting grin as he went by, I thought I would not detain him. He was hardly gone when I heard the clacking again, and another one issued from the shadowy half-light. This one was bending under a heavy gravestone, and dragging a shabby coffin after him by a string. When he got to me he gave me a steady look for a moment or two, and then rounded to and backed up to me, saying:

"Ease this down for a fellow, will you?"

I eased the gravestone down till it rested on the ground, and in doing so noticed that it bore the name of "John Baxter Cop-

[1] Written about 1870.

manhurst," with "May, 1839," as the date of his death. Deceased sat wearily down by me, and wiped his os frontis with his major maxillary—chiefly from former habit I judged, for I could not see that he brought away any perspiration.

"It is too bad, too bad," said he, drawing the remnant of the shroud about him and leaning his jaw pensively on his hand. Then he put his left foot up on his knee and fell to scratching his ankle-bone absently with a rusty nail which he got out of his coffin.

"What is too bad, friend?"

"Oh, everything, everything. I almost wish I never had died."

"You surprise me. Why do you say this? Has anything gone wrong? What is the matter?"

"Matter! Look at this shroud—rags. Look at this gravestone, all battered up. Look at that disgraceful old coffin. All a man's property going to ruin and destruction before his eyes, and ask him if anything is wrong? Fire and brimstone!"

"Calm yourself, calm yourself," I said. "It *is* too bad—it is certainly too bad, but then I had not supposed that you would much mind such matters, situated as you are."

"Well, my dear sir, I *do* mind them. My pride is hurt, and my comfort is impaired—destroyed, I might say. I will state my case—I will put it to you in such a way that you can comprehend it, if you will let me," said the poor skeleton, tilting the hood of his shroud back, as if he were clearing for action, and thus unconsciously giving himself a jaunty and festive air very much at variance with the grave character of his position in life—so to speak—and in prominent contrast with his distressful mood.

"Proceed," said I.

"I reside in the shameful old graveyard a block or two above you here, in this street—there, now, I just expected that cartilage would let go!—third rib from the bottom, friend, hitch the end of it to my spine with a string, if you have got such a thing about you, though a bit of silver wire is a deal pleasanter, and more durable and becoming, if one keeps it polished—to think of shredding out and going to pieces in this way, just on account of the indifference and neglect of one's posterity!"—and the poor ghost grated his teeth in a way that gave me a wrench and a shiver—for the effect is mightily increased by the absence of muffling flesh and cuticle. "I reside in that old graveyard, and have for these thirty years; and I tell you things are changed since I first laid this old tired frame there, and turned over, and stretched out for a long sleep, with a delicious sense upon me of being *done* with bother, and grief, and anxiety, and doubt, and fear, forever and ever, and listening with comfortable and increasing satisfaction to the sexton's work, from the startling clatter of his first spadeful on my coffin till it dulled away to the faint patting that shaped the roof of my new home—delicious!" My! I wish you could try it to-night!" and out of my reverie deceased fetched me a rattling slap with a bony hand.

"Yes, sir, thirty years ago I laid me down there, and was happy. For it was out in the country then—out in the breezy, flowery, grand old woods, and the lazy winds gossiped with the leaves, and the squirrels capered over us and around us, and the creeping things visited us, and the birds filled the tranquil solitude with music. Ah, it was worth ten years of a man's life to be dead then! Everything was pleasant. I was in a good neighborhood, for all the dead people that lived near me belonged to the best families in the city. Our posterity appeared to think the world of us. They kept our graves in the very best condition; the fences were always in faultless repair, headboards were kept painted or whitewashed, and were replaced with new ones as soon as they began to look rusty or decayed; monuments were kept upright, railings intact and bright, the rose-bushes and shrubbery trimmed, trained, and free from blemish, the walks clean and smooth and graveled. But that day is gone by. Our descendants have forgotten us. My grandson lives in a stately house built with money made by these old hands of mine, and I sleep in a neglected grave with invading vermin that gnaw my shroud to build them nests withal! I and friends that lie with me founded and secured the prosperity of this fine city, and the stately bantling of our loves leaves us to rot in a dilapidated cemetery which neighbors curse and strangers scoff at. See the difference between the old time and this—for instance: Our graves are all caved in now; our headboards have rotted away and tumbled down; our railings reel this way and that, with one foot in the air, after a fashion of unseemly levity; our monuments lean wearily, and our gravestones bow their heads discouraged; there be no adornments any more—no roses, nor shrubs, nor graveled walks, nor anything that is a comfort to the eye; and even the paintless old board fence that did make a show of holding us sacred from companionship with beasts and the defilement of heedless feet, has tottered till it overhangs the street, and only advertises the presence of our dismal resting-place and invites yet more derision to it. And now we cannot hide our poverty and tatters in the friendly woods, for the city has stretched its withering arms abroad and taken us in, and all that remains of the cheer of our old home is the cluster of lugubrious forest trees that stand, bored and weary of a city life, with their feet in our coffins, looking into the hazy distance and wishing they were there. I tell you it is disgraceful!

"You begin to comprehend—you begin to see how it is. While our descendants are living sumptuously on our money, right around us in the city, we have to fight hard to keep skull and bones together. Bless you, there isn't a grave in our cemetery that doesn't leak—not one. Every time it rains in the night we have to climb out and roost in the trees—and sometimes we are wakened suddenly by the chilly water trickling down the back of our necks. Then I tell you there is a general heaving up of old graves and kicking over of old monuments, and scampering of old skeletons for the trees! Bless me, if you had gone along there some such nights after twelve you might have seen as many as fifteen of us roosting on one limb, with our joints rattling drearily and the wind wheezing through our ribs! Many a time we have perched there for three or four dreary hours, and then come down, stiff and chilled through and drowsy, and borrowed each other's skulls to bail out our graves with—if you will glance up in my mouth now as I tilt my head back, you can see that my head-piece is half full of old dry sediment—how top-heavy and stupid it makes me sometimes! Yes, sir, many a time if you had happened to come along just before the dawn you'd have caught us bailing out the graves and hanging our shrouds on the fence to dry. Why, I had an elegant shroud stolen from there one morning—think a party by the name of Smith took it, that resides in a plebeian graveyard over yonder—I think so because the first time I ever saw him he hadn't anything on but a check shirt, and the last time I saw him, which was at a social gathering in the new cemetery, he was the best-dressed corpse in the company—and it is a significant fact that he left when he saw me; and presently an old woman from here missed her coffin—she generally took it with her when she went anywhere, because she was liable to take cold and bring on the spasmodic rheumatism that originally killed her if she exposed herself to the night air much. She was named Hotchkiss — Anna Matilda Hotchkiss — you might know her? She has two upper front teeth, is tall, but a good deal inclined to stoop, one rib on the left side gone, has one shred of rusty hair hanging from the left side of her head, and one little tuft just above and a little forward of her right ear, has her underjaw wired on one side where it had worked loose, small bone of left forearm gone—lost in a fight—has a kind of swagger in her gait and a 'gallus' way of going with her arms akimbo and her nostrils in the air—has been pretty free and easy, and is all damaged and battered up till she looks like a queensware crate in ruins—maybe you have met her?"

"God forbid!" I involuntarily ejaculated, for somehow I was not looking for that form of question, and it caught me a little off my guard. But I hastened to make amends for my rudeness, and say, "I simply meant I had not had the honor—for I would not deliberately speak discourteously of a friend of yours. You were saying that you were robbed—and it was a shame, too—but it appears by what is left of the shroud you have on that it was a costly one in its day. How did—"

A most ghastly expression began to develop among the decayed features and shriveled integuments of my guest's face, and I was beginning to grow uneasy and distressed, when he told me he was only working up a deep, sly smile, with a wink in it, to suggest that about the time he acquired his present garment a ghost in a neighboring cemetery missed one. This reassured me, but I begged him to confine himself to speech thenceforth, because his facial expression was uncertain. Even with the most elaborate care it was liable to miss fire. Smiling should especially be avoided. What *he* might honestly consider a shining success was likely to strike me in a very different light. I said I liked to see a skeleton cheerful, even decorously playful, but I did not think smiling was a skeleton's best hold.

"Yes, friend," said the poor skeleton, "the facts are just as I have given them to you. Two of these old graveyards—the one that I resided in and one further along—have been deliberately neglected by our descendants of today until there is no occupying them any longer. Aside from the osteological discomfort of it—and that is no light matter this rainy weather—the present state of things is ruinous to property. We have got to move or be content to see our effects wasted away and utterly destroyed. Now, you will hardly believe it, but it is true, nevertheless, that there isn't a single coffin in good repair among all my acquaintance—now that is an absolute fact. I do not refer to low people who come in a pine box mounted on an express-wagon, but I am talking about your high-toned, silver-mounted burial-case, your monumental sort, that travel under black plumes at the head of a procession and have choice of cemetery lots—I mean folks like the Jarvises, and the Bledsoes and Burlings, and such. They are all about ruined. The most substantial people in our set, they were. And now look at them—utterly used up and poverty-stricken. One of the Bledsoes actually traded his monument to a late barkeeper for some fresh shavings to put under his head. I tell you it speaks volumes, for there is nothing a corpse takes so much pride in as his monument. He loves to read the inscription. He comes after a while to believe what it says himself, and then you may see him sitting on the fence night after night enjoying it. Epitaphs are cheap, and they do a poor chap a world of good after he is dead, especially if he had hard luck while he was alive. I wish they were used more. Now I don't complain, but confidentially I *do* think it was a little shabby in my descendants to give me nothing but this old slab of a gravestone—and all the more that there isn't a compliment on it. It used to have

'GONE TO HIS JUST REWARD'

on it, and I was proud when I first saw it, but by and by I noticed that whenever an old friend of mine came along he would hook his chin on the railing and pull a long face and read along down till he came to that, and then he would chuckle to himself and walk off, looking satisfied and comfortable. So I scratched it off to get rid of those fools. But a dead man always takes a deal of pride in his monument. Yonder goes half a dozen of the Jarvises now, with the family monument along. And Smithers and some hired specters went by with his awhile ago. Hello, Higgins, good-by, old friend! That's Meredith Higgins—died in '44—belongs to our set in the cemetery—fine old family—great-grandmother was an Injun—I am on the most familiar terms with him—he didn't hear me was the reason he didn't answer me. And I am sorry, too, because I would have liked to introduce you. You would admire him. He is the most disjointed, sway-backed, and generally distorted old skeleton you ever saw, but he is full of fun. When he laughs it sounds like rasping two stones together, and he always starts it off with a cheery screech like raking a nail across a window-pane. Hey, Jones! That is old Columbus Jones—shroud cost four hundred dollars—entire trousseau, including monument, twenty-seven hundred. This was in the spring of '26. It was enormous style for those days. Dead people came all the way from the Alleghanies to see his things—the party that occupied the grave next to mine remembers it well. Now do you see that individual going along with a piece of a head-board under his arm, one leg-bone below his knee gone, and not a thing in the world on? That is Barstow Dalhousie, and next to Columbus Jones he was the most sumptuously outfitted person that ever entered our cemetery. We are all leaving. We cannot tolerate the treatment we are receiving at the hands of our descendants. They open new cemeteries, but they leave us to our ignominy. They mend the streets, but they never mend anything that is about us or belongs to us. Look at that coffin of mine—yet I tell you in its day it was a piece of furniture that would have attracted attention in any drawing-room in this city. You may have it if you want it—I can't afford to repair it. Put a new bottom in her, and part of a new top, and a bit of fresh lining along the left side, and you'll find her about as comfortable as any receptacle of her species you ever tried. No thanks—no, don't mention it—you have been civil to me, and I would give you all the property I have got before I would seem ungrateful. Now this winding-sheet is a kind of a sweet thing in its way, if you would like to— No? Well, just as you say, but I wished to be fair and liberal—there's nothing mean about *me*. Good-by, friend, I must be going. I may have a good way to go tonight —don't know. I only know one thing for certain, and that is that I am on the emigrant trail now, and I'll never sleep in that crazy old cemetery again. I will travel till I find respectable quarters, if I have to hoof it to New Jersey. All the boys are going. It was decided in public conclave, last night, to emigrate, and by the time the sun rises there won't be a bone left in our old habitations. Such cemeteries may suit my surviving friends, but they do not suit the remains that have the honor to make these remarks. My opinion is the general opinion. If you doubt it, go and see how the departing ghosts upset things before they started. They were almost riotous in their demonstrations of distaste. Hello, here are some of the Bledsoes, and if you will give me a lift with this tombstone I guess I will join company and jog along with them—mighty respectable old family, the

Bledsoes, and used to always come out in six-horse hearses and all that sort of thing fifty years ago when I walked these streets in daylight. Good-by, friend."

And with his gravestone on his shoulder he joined the grisly procession, dragging his damaged coffin after him, for notwithstanding he pressed it upon me so earnestly, I utterly refused his hospitality. I suppose that for as much as two hours these sad outcasts went clacking by, laden with their dismal effects, and all that time I sat pitying them. One or two of the youngest and least dilapidated among them inquired about midnight trains on the railways, but the rest seemed unacquainted with that mode of travel, and merely asked about common public roads to various towns and cities, some of which are not on the map now, and vanished from it and from the earth as much as thirty years ago, and some few of them never *had* existed anywhere but on maps, and private ones in real-estate agencies at that. And they asked about the condition of the cemeteries in these towns and cities, and about the reputation the citizens bore as to reverence for the dead.

This whole matter interested me deeply, and likewise compelled my sympathy for these homeless ones. And it all seeming real, and I not knowing it was a dream, I mentioned to one shrouded wanderer an idea that had entered my head to publish an account of this curious and very sorrowful exodus, but said also that I could not describe it truthfully, and just as it occurred, without seeming to trifle with a grave subject and exhibit an irreverence for the dead that would shock and distress their surviving friends. But this bland and stately remnant of a former citizen leaned him far over my gate and whispered in my ear, and said:

"Do not let that disturb you. The community that can stand such graveyards as those we are emigrating from can stand anything a body can say about the neglected and forsaken dead that lie in them."

At that very moment a cock crowed, and the weird procession vanished and left not a shred or a bone behind. I awoke, and found myself lying with my head out of the bed and "sagging" downward considerably—a position favorable to dreaming dreams with morals in them, maybe, but not poetry.

NOTE.—The reader is assured that if the cemeteries in his town are kept in good order, this Dream is not leveled at his town at all, but is leveled particularly and venomously at the *next* town.

THE PETRIFIED MAN

NOW, to show how really hard it is to foist a moral or a truth upon an unsuspecting public through a burlesque without entirely and absurdly missing one's mark, I will here set down two experiences of my own in this thing. In the fall of 1862, in Nevada and California, the people got to running wild about extraordinary petrifactions and other natural marvels. One could scarcely pick up a paper without finding in it one or two glorified discoveries of this kind. The mania was becoming a little ridiculous. I was a brand-new local editor in Virginia City, and I felt called upon to destroy this growing evil; we all have our benignant, fatherly moods at one time or another, I suppose. I chose to kill the petrifaction mania with a delicate, a very delicate satire. But maybe it was altogether too delicate, for nobody ever perceived the satire part of it at all. I put my scheme in the shape of the discovery of a remarkably petrified man.

I had had a temporary falling out with Mr. ——, the new coroner and justice of the peace of Humboldt, and thought I might as well touch him up a little at the same time and make him ridiculous, and thus combine pleasure with business. So I told, in patient, belief-compelling detail, all about the finding of a petrified man at Gravelly Ford (exactly a hundred and twenty miles, over a breakneck mountain trail from where —— lived); how all the savants of the immediate neighborhood had been to examine it (it was notorious that there was not a living creature within fifty miles of there, except a few starving Indians, some crippled grasshoppers, and four or five buzzards out of meat and too feeble to get away); how those savants all pronounced the petrified man to have been in a state of complete petrifaction for over ten generations; and then, with a seriousness that I ought to have been ashamed to assume, I stated that as soon as Mr. —— heard the news he summoned a jury, mounted his mule, and posted off, with noble reverence for official duty, on that awful five days' journey, through alkali, sagebrush, peril of body, and imminent starvation, to *hold an inquest* on this man that had been dead and turned to everlasting stone for more than three hundred years! And then, my hand being "in," so to speak, I went on, with the same unflinching gravity, to state that the jury returned a verdict that deceased came to his death from *protracted exposure*. This only moved me to higher flights of imagination, and I said that the jury, with that charity so characteristic of pioneers, then dug a grave, and were about to give the petrified man Christian burial, when they found that for ages a limestone sediment had been trickling down the face of the stone against which he was sitting, and this stuff had run under him and cemented him fast to the "bed-rock"; that the jury (they were all silver-miners) canvassed the difficulty a moment, and then got out their powder and fuse, and proceeded to drill a hole under him, in order to *blast him from his position*, when Mr. ——, "with that delicacy so characteristic of him, forbade them, observing that it would be little less than sacrilege to do such a thing."

From beginning to end the "Petrified Man" squib was a string of roaring absurdities, albeit they were told with an unfair pretense of truth that even imposed upon me to some extent, and I was in some danger of believing in my own fraud. But I really had no desire to deceive anybody, and no expectation of doing it. I depended on the way the petrified man was *sitting* to explain to the public that he was a swindle. Yet I purposely mixed that up with other things, hoping to make it obscure—and I did. I would describe the position of one foot, and then say his right thumb was against the side of his nose; then talk about his other foot, and presently come back and say the fingers of his right hand were spread apart; then talk about the back of his head a little, and return and say the left thumb was hooked into the right little finger; then ramble off about something else, and by and by drift back again and remark that the fingers of the left hand were spread like those of the right. But I was too ingenious. I mixed it up rather too much; and so all that description of the attitude, as a key to the humbuggery of the article, was entirely lost, for nobody but me ever discovered and comprehended the peculiar and suggestive position of the petrified man's hands.

As a *satire* on the petrifaction mania, or anything else, my Petrified Man was a disheartening failure; for everybody received him in innocent good faith, and I was stunned to see the creature I had begotten to pull down the wonder-business with, and bring derision upon it, calmly exalted to the grand chief place in the list of the genuine marvels our Nevada had produced. I was so disappointed at the curious miscarriage of my scheme, that at first I was angry, and did not like to think about it; but by and by, when the exchanges began to come in with the Petrified Man copied and guilelessly glorified, I began to feel a soothing secret satisfaction; and as my gentleman's field of travels broadened, and by the exchanges I saw that he steadily and implacably penetrated territory after territory, state after state, and land after land, till he swept the great globe and culminated in sublime and unimpeached legitimacy in the august London *Lancet,* my cup was full, and I said I was glad I had done it. I think that for about eleven months, as nearly as I can remember, Mr. ——'s daily mail-bag continued to be swollen by the addition of half a bushel of newspapers hailing from many climes with the Petrified Man in them, marked around with a prominent belt of ink. I sent them to him. I did it for spite, not for fun. He used to shovel them into his back yard and curse. And every day during all those months the miners, his constituents (for miners never quit joking a person when they get started), would call on him and ask if he could tell them where they could get hold of a paper with the Petrified Man in it. He could have accommodated a continent with them. I hated —— in those days, and these things pacified me and pleased me. I could not have gotten more real comfort out of him without killing him.

MARK TWAIN WRITES TO AMUSE HIS MOTHER

To Jane Clemens, in Keokuk:

Elmira, August 7, 1886

Dear Ma,

I heard that Molly and Orion and Pamela had been sick, but I see by your letter that they are much better now, or nearly well. When we visited you a month ago, it seemed to us that your Keokuk weather was pretty hot; Jean and Clara sat up in bed at Mrs. McElroy's and cried about it, and so did I; but I judge by your letter that it has cooled down, now, so that a person is comparatively comfortable, with his skin off. Well, it did need cooling; I remember that I burnt a hole in my shirt, there, with some ice cream that fell on it; and Miss Jenkins told me they never used a stove, but cooked their meals on a marble-topped table in the drawing-room, just with the natural heat. If anybody else had told me, I would not have believed it. I was told by the Bishop of Keokuk that he did not allow crying at funerals, because it scalded the furniture. If Miss Jenkins had told me that I would have believed it. This reminds me that you speak of Dr. Jenkins and his family as if they were strangers to me. Indeed they are not. Don't you suppose I remember gratefully how tender the doctor was with Jean when she hurt her arm, and how quickly he got the pain out of the hurt, whereas I supposed it was going to last at least an hour? No, I don't forget some things as easily as I do others.

Yes, it was pretty hot weather. Now here, when a person is going to die, he is always in a sweat about where he is going to; but in Keokuk of course they don't care, because they are fixed for everything. It has set me reflecting, it has taught me a lesson. By and by, when my health fails, I am going to put all my affairs in order, and bid good-bye to my friends here, and kill all the people I don't like, and go out to Keokuk and prepare for death.

They are all well in this family, and we all send love.

Affly Your Son

SAM

ORDER FROM YOUR FAVORITE BOOKSELLER OR CALL FOR OUR FREE CATALOG

***The New Revelation: The Coming of a New Spiritual Paradigm,* by Arthur Conan Doyle.** Arthur Conan Doyle was a famous mystery writer (*The Adventures of Sherlock Holmes*) and spiritualist from the early twentieth century who predicted, with this book, the coming of a spiritually based religion in the future. This "New Revelation" seems to have taken shape. as he had predicted, in the form of the New Age Movement. Doyle based this book on the spiritualist movement of his day which included channeling, seances, automatic writing, and a variety of other strange, psychic occurrences. He investigated these things thoroughly and came away convinced that more proof existed within these realms than could be found within any standard religion. He acknowledged some of the fraudulent scams that were exposed in spiritual circles and stated that serious researchers like himself completely deplored such events and that they were not representative of the larger areas of authentic psychic phenomena. As our more modern research continues, we may be able to clear up some of the deeper mysteries concerning who we are and where we go after death. If this should happen it would truly qualify as a "new revelation", one that would shake our religious foundations to the core. The "Old Revelation", Doyle says, has lost its power through bigotry, mismanagement, materialism, and claims of infallibility that no longer hold up. A new world of personal discovery awaits us, as an alternative, and one can begin to explore it now by reading this classic work. **ISBN 1-58509-220-7 • 124 pages • 6 x 9 • trade paper • $12.95**

***A Short History of the World,* by H.G. Wells.** This is a book for the average person with a great curiosity of the world. H.G. Wells had an intense curiosity and used it to investigate and then share the entire history of the world in a condensed form. Wells, the great science fiction writer who wrote *The War of the Worlds* and *The Invisible Man*, among others, was fascinated with the real world just as much as his imaginary ones. This book is a testament to his genius and immense knowledge involving the key events of humanity throughout the history of the world. It is true that much was left out, but Wells covers the high points so that one can follow the more important paths of history as we learned, grew, and reached deeper understandings throughout our physical, intellectual, and spiritual evolution. The great thing about this book is that it allows us to see a bigger picture. An overall pattern emerges that one can only grasp by reading and experiencing the book fully. Wells was considered a genius and clearly wrote with this larger vision in mind. Upon completing the book he reveals that we, as humanity, are still in our infancy and have only just begun an immense and important journey. The pattern he lays out shows that we are moving toward new ways of understanding, growth, and wisdom. This book should be read by those who wish to understand more about our place in the world. **ISBN 1-58509-211-8 • 320 pages • 6 x 9 • trade paper • $24.95**

The Voyages and Discoveries of the Companions of Columbus by Washington Irving. Washington Irving is known to have been one of the greatest and most interesting writers who ever lived. In addition to having written *Rip Van Winkle* and *The Legend of Sleepy Hollow*, he wrote two books on early seafarers and the exploration of the world. The first, *The Life and Voyages of Christopher Columbus*, provides a fascinating view of Columbus and has been found in print in recent years. This book, however, is far more rare. Written in 1835, it may well have been lost to history had a surviving copy not been found in a small New England antique shop. We consider this book more exciting than his work on Columbus because most everyone knows that story. New lands were waiting to be discovered, explored, and claimed. The excitement brims from this book as the floodgates were newly opened and various explorers set out in search of fame and to experience some of the greatest adventures that the world has ever known. Famous explorers profiled include Balboa, Alonzo de Ojeda, Amerigo Vespucci, whom America was named after, and Ponce de Leon, who was searching for the fountain of youth. An interesting part of the book is found in the Appendix, where Irving reproduces the *Manifesto of Alonzo de Ojeda*. This message to the natives was read aloud by Spanish friars shortly before Ojeda's attack on those "savages" at Carthenega. It starts out rather politely, but finishes by demanding their allegiance to becoming Christians and Spanish subjects, or else die. This manifesto later became adopted by all Spanish discoverers, and is a very important piece of history. The book itself is a gold mine of valuable information. **ISBN 1-58509-500-1 • 352 pages • 6 x 9 • hard cover • $39.95**

***Reason and Belief: The Impact of Scientific Discovery on Religious and Spiritual Faith,* by Sir Oliver Lodge.** Sir Oliver Lodge was a respected writer from the early twentieth century. At this time, there were a number of scientific advances that caused one to consider the ramifications of these new discoveries on the religious and spiritual beliefs of the day. But the impact of science may not be so great on spiritual matters in the final analysis, according to Lodge. He puts forth a number of interesting examples. He does not champion science as the final answer, which is what makes this book so interesting. Science is still helpful. It is a tool that is allowing us to reach spiritual answers that have so far not been found. Lodge actively searches for spiritual answers with great wisdom throughout the book and, when necessary, backs off from his great spiritual knowledge and explores our grasp of science to help us along. The last third of the book covers the scope of science. Lodge is a mystic who states that science is useful, but will never embrace the whole of knowledge. Thinking that science is and will be the final answer is the mistake in thinking that scientists of today fall into. They often ignore the seers and prophets of the past who have given us great spiritual truths. Scientists depend solely on a limited bandwidth of discipline that sometimes creates blinders, as found on a racehorse that can only run in a straight line. If the answer is off to the side, as part of the infinite world around us, it will never be seen. Lodge takes the blinders off, and opens us up to the larger possibilities around us. **ISBN 1-58509-226-6 • 180 pages • 6 x 9 • trade paper • $17.95**

***William Blake: A Biography,* by Basil De Selincourt.** William Blake was a great painter, poet, and mystic who rejected science and reason and preferred using the powers of imagination in his quest for truth. Because of his psychological and visionary views, he was considered a forerunner to Freud and Carl Jung. He was a Christian who also developed a belief in many Gods, giving names to them and drawing their images. They often took the roles of Jung's archetypes, or unconscious patterns from within the human mind that are common to all people. The visions he experienced came to him spontaneously, and much of his poetry was "dictated" from some kind of spiritual realm. His genius was best represented in his ability to create myths. They seemed to function within a Christian framework, as Blake grew up heavily influenced by Swedenborg. The Swedenborgian "new church" was believed to have started in an inner world or "in the heavens" in 1757, the same year that Blake was born. This is a book that outlines Blake's interesting life. Some people thought him to be utterly mad; others considered him a genius. One thing is certain—this biography will not be boring to those interested in the bold adventures of a man who spent his life as a spiritual pioneer. **ISBN 1-58509-225-8 • 384 pages • 6 x 9 • trade paper • $28.95**

***Crux Ansata: An Indictment of the Roman Catholic Church,* by H. G. Wells.** When most people think of the great H. G. Wells what comes to mind are his science fiction books like *The War of the Worlds, The Invisible Man*, and others. Yet Wells was a brilliant man who was deeply interested in history and current events. He wrote this book at the height of World War II, just after he had resigned as Minister of Allied Propaganda. While in this position he became privy to information that totally shocked him concerning the Roman Catholic Church. Much of what he found is in this book. This book is clearly an indictment of the Roman Catholic church, as stated in the subtitle, not only based on what Wells had discovered during the war, but on his research of the Church throughout its entire existence. After this book was released a loud protest was issued from the Roman Catholic press accusing Wells, a respected writer and researcher, of spreading half-truths, innuendoes, and logical fallacies. Wells responded by saying that the church routinely engages in a complex, modern boycott of liberal thought that requires us to fight this intolerance with our own intolerance of the Roman Catholic system. This book has been swept under the rug of history, for the most part, because Wells was a famous person who openly and vocally questioned the status quo. Mark Twain is another good example—who wrote radical criticisms along religious lines, but publishers quietly sweep them aside and hope no one will look. **ISBN 1-58509-210-X • 160 pages • 6 x 9 • trade paper • $14.95**

---

www.ingramcontent.com/pod-product-compliance
Lightning Source LLC
Chambersburg PA
CBHW020145180626
46810CB00004B/1737
* 9 7 8 1 5 8 5 0 9 2 0 0 0 *